Mona,

Live large,
laugh loud, love
deep & enjoy
everything.

Linda

The Kiss 💋

Linda C

Copyright © 2004 by Linda Chimenti

ISBN 0-7414-2219-0

Published by:

INFINITY
PUBLISHING.COM

1094 New DeHaven Street, Suite 100
West Conshohocken, PA 19428-2713
Info@buybooksontheweb.com
www.buybooksontheweb.com
Toll-free (877) BUY BOOK
Local Phone (610) 941-9999
Fax (610) 941-9959

Printed in the United States of America

Printed on Recycled Paper

Published September 2004

ILLUSION: An erroneous perception of reality.

Is it possible that our need to be loved as humans is so strong that we are willing to do anything for even a glimpse of this love?

Or

Is it because we need to be closer to our Creator that we search for this love? Is this the reason that even a hint of love feels so wonderful?

These glimpses are short lived for most and their beauty feels like an *illusion;* is this because we are human?

THE KISS

I met a beautiful woman with red hair and green eyes. Her smile could light up a room and her heart was sweet. We became friends and my life was forever changed.

She told me a story about a kiss. 💋

This kiss was no ordinary kiss; it was so romantic and so tender that it altered her life in an instant.

It was a magical kiss. 💋 They sometimes are!

The story of that kiss was just the beginning of the stories she shared with me during our friendship. With each disclosure her soul became closer to being set free; and I learned a lot about the human heart.

This is her story.

💋   💋   💋   💋

Chapter 1

I remember the date, day and hour when I lost my virginity. It was a beautiful spring night, ten thirty three, Wednesday. My soft yellow dress was moving gently against my slim body in the temperate spring breeze as I stood in the shopping center parking lot waiting for Jack to arrive. I was nervously smoking a cigarette and considering changing my mind when the limousine pulled up. Jack got out and politely helped me into the backseat and then joined me there before giving instructions to the driver to proceed.

The limousine slowly exited the parking lot and moved easily along Wisconsin Avenue in the manageable late night traffic. Jack did not say much to me, he knew that I was nervous. He handed me a glass of champagne and smiled his wonderful warm smile. He had removed his suit jacket and tie and his soft blue dress shirt was unbuttoned at the collar. After sipping champagne my body started to relax. I moved myself into a less rigid position on the seat placing my legs across Jack's lap.

I can still remember the cool leather seats in the limousine and the way the drivers eyes watched us in the mirror. I can still conjure up memories of Jack's cologne and the feel of his soft hands as they gently moved along my legs up over my thighs and removed my panties. I could feel the excitement in my body and I could hear my heart pounding. I knew I was about to commit a mortal sin but my rebellion was stronger than my guilt and I felt free.

Up till this point in my life I had had a few boyfriends, nothing serious just the usual high school infatuations. The first boy I kissed was Jimmy, a pretty good kisser for someone who was only fifteen at the time. We had known each other since elementary school and I think we were both just experimenting, feeling our way through the raging hormones of adolescence.

Then there was Steve, my official first boyfriend. He was very sweet and his dark black hair and green eyes made him so handsome. We fooled around but never actually had intercourse. Steve's father was in the service and the family had to move to Denver after our first few months together. I missed him a lot, I cried daily for a while, but as time passed I slowly pushed his memory below the surface and moved on.

Finally there was Nick, who had dropped out of high school and worked at the local gas station. Hip, slick and cool in every way. I was crazy about him. Being a rebellious teenager there wasn't anything that brought me more joy than the look on my mother's face when he would bring me home from school in his old Dodge convertible. Nick made me laugh a lot but I somehow intuitively knew he was not the one I wanted to make love to for the first time.

I wanted that first time to be special. Something memorable. Something monumental.

I had carefully searched out the man who would be the one, the one who would give this gift of love to me. When I met Jack I knew he was the one. I was not in love with him; I just knew that he was the one. Women sincerely liked Jack. They would come by to talk and laugh with him, touching him, caressing him. He had a smile that was so light and warm. His hands were beautiful with long fingers, manicured nails, the kind of hands you want touching you, holding your ass as he pulled you into him.

I was young, eighteen, just a few days past my birthday, he was thirty seven and I imagined that he was an expert at the art of making love. I don't remember exactly how we ended up in the limousine, how it actually happened, but I do remember that I had planned it would be him and him alone that would penetrate me for the first time, the time that counted most, the time that all other times would be measured against.

Jack was so gentle with me, as I leaned back in the seat; I could smell the leather mixed with his cologne, it was intoxicating, exciting. I raised my feet up onto the seat and parted my legs. Jack then ran his hands up over my young thighs, I shivered with excitement. He then slipped into me without too much effort, I was so wet. This was an incredible new sensation. I felt connected. Pleasure consumed me. He moved slowly in and out of me for a while and then lifted my small body onto his lap pulling me down onto him. The pleasure was so intense that my head fell backwards and my back arched, my small breasts lifted up and my nipples were hard. After what seemed like a long time Jack had an orgasm, time stopped, he let out a long groan as I screamed in ecstasy and slumped forward, my head coming to rest on his shoulder.

When Jack released his hold on me I laid back on the seat watching his face, the face of a man who was kind and gentle, the face of a man who was pleasured by his satisfaction and mine. As I watched Jack's face a significant thought came to me, I realized that we had not actually made love, we had had sex, and I liked it very much. I was peaceful, I felt beautiful, I felt as if I had grown up.

I don't think we said a thing to each other until we uttered the words "goodbye" when he dropped me back at my car. My head swirled from the champagne we sipped. Yes, I was high on the champagne but more so I was high on the sex. It was intoxicating, just as the champagne was intoxicating, just as that first sip of Seagram's out of the pint bottle was intoxicating, just as marijuana was intoxicating.

I was hooked.

I knew I would see him again, he was my boss. Jack would be there when I arrived at work the next day. We never talked about the incident, ever, we just acted as though its time had come and gone and things were just the way they always were. But they weren't because I was different, I had left the world of little girl things and entered a world of grown up things. I would never be the same. I could never go back. My new world would not be like the safety of the limousine it would be filled with adventure and fear, pleasure and pain, lies and secrets, illusions and delusions.

I was hooked.

And I wanted more.

Chapter 2

Now that I had actually managed to lose my virginity before graduation I knew it would be a wonderful summer. Saying goodbye to all my classmates was more of a relief than anything else. I had gone to school with most of them since elementary school and I really wanted to get away from them and all the things they represented. I wanted to live the life I read about in magazines. I wanted so much more than the suburban life I lived. I wanted so much more than my mother had. I guess I just wanted more.

Not long after my experience with Jack I met a man at a nightclub. Paul was in his thirties and was very handsome. Nice ass, long dark hair, beautiful lips, kissable lips. He sent me a glass of champagne and when I smiled and glanced at him he came over to where I was seated and asked me to dance. We danced and drank and laughed and a few hours later he took me to his home. I was a little intoxicated but I remember walking into the lobby of one of the prettiest apartment buildings I had ever been in. Paul made a gesture at the security guard and pulled me onto the elevator. As the elevator doors closed he pressed me against the mirrored wall and lifted up my dress to expose my lace panties, he stared at me in the mirror until the doors opened on the seventeenth floor. He then lifted me up gently and carried me to his apartment.

Once inside he wasted no time on formalities, he just carried me to his bed and set me down as if I were a precious package. I was excited and a little afraid. I let him take the lead and I just laid there on his huge bed. The room was dark except for some dim lights. The ceiling over the bed was covered with mirrors and I could see myself lying on the bed.

Paul told me not to move and he would be right back, he left the room. I sat there like a statue, scanning around the room with my eyes. The furniture was black lacquer with gold trim. The drapes matched the bedspread which was red velvet and he had a leather chair next to the bed. The soft light radiated from an opening in the drapes that exposed a view of the city lights.

I heard voices outside of the bedroom and then the door opened and Paul came in carrying his favorite drink, vodka/orange juice/Seven Up. He had a joint between his lips and was fumbling with the lighter as he closed the door with his foot. He sat on the bed next to me and offered me a toke off the joint and a sip of his drink.

He laid down next to me on the bed slowing drawing on the joint and inhaling deeply as he handed it to me. I too, took a long slow deep hit and relaxed as the intoxicating effects took over my body and my mind. The marijuana made me thirsty and I needed a gulp of his drink, it was refreshing and awful at the same time. Alcohol for me was always a cut to the chase of where I wanted to be, I never liked anything in my alcohol, not even ice, let alone the contaminants of orange juice and Seven Up.

As I sipped his drink the vodka took over and my fears evaporated. I loved this feeling, the feeling of not really being here, feelings that had blurry edges. We sat there for what seemed like a long time, my dress pulled up around my waist exposing my thin hips and lace panties. My beautiful young legs were slighting parted and my high heels were still on my feet. I could not help looking at myself in the mirrors above the bed, I felt so pretty laying there on the red velvet with this handsome man next to me, my skin glistening in the dim lights, my head so light, so free. Paul was still fully dressed except for his bare feet.

With a sudden quick movement Paul rolled off the huge bed. He stood next to the leather chair and unbuttoned his silk shirt exposing his dark smooth skin. He had a beautiful body; it looked as though he worked out, not much, just enough to keep him trim and shapely. I watched his every move. My head swirled. I was so taken by his gentleness, his purposeful moves. His confidence; I had never felt confident. I did not feel like the woman he appeared to be seeing. I did not believe I was desirable to a man like him. He removed his belt, unfastened the hook, slowly pulled the zipper down and stepped carefully out of his pants, which he laid neatly over the back of the leather chair. He was more beautiful at that moment than I ever remembered again, and I was so excited by this vision that I could feel the wetness between my legs. I shifted on to my side facing him calling to him with my eyes, wanting so much to feel his hands on my body, his lips on my neck, my nipples hardened, I reached between my legs to calm the exhilaration that I was feeling. He then removed his shirt, laid it over the chair and crawled across the bed slowly towards me. The anticipation of his touch was so exciting I could feel my body start to spasm and my hips rose off the bed as I rolled onto my back, my eyes closed and I could feel the excitement pumping through my veins.

He placed his hand on my ankle and slowing ran it up my leg, past my knee, over my thigh, and put his finger into my vagina, I screamed with pleasure. The scream sounded like it came from somewhere else. A scream so intense and so alien to me. I had never felt this level of pleasure; a pleasure derived from anticipation. It was intoxicating. I felt like the most beautiful woman in the world. I felt as though pleasure was mine to have and enjoy. I did not know at that moment that I would search out this pleasure in the future and take all that I desired. I did not know that this pleasure would have a very high price, and that I would pay for this pleasure over and over. All that mattered at that moment was the pleasure I was feeling and I wanted more.

I wanted more.

We had sex for hours. Hours of pleasure. Hours of intoxication. When I finally lay back from exhaustion I could see myself in the mirror, high heels still on, hair wet against my face, skin shiny from my sweat and his. Paul was laying in a fetal position across the bottom of the bed, his long dark hair tangled and wet. I heard a few whimpers then silence, heavy breathing, sleep had taken over. I did not want to sleep. Excitement still pulsed through every cell of my body. My mind raced. I did eventually fall asleep for an hour or so. The next morning Paul had to work and he had his roommate Philip drive me back to the club where I had left my car.

Chapter 3

My relationship with Paul was intense from the beginning until it ended in a very ugly way some five years later. There were so many things about Paul that I never understood and that I would not have figured out then because I was so naïve so young so innocent. But as I look back on it now, it was better that way. I had many experiences due to my innocence and my total trust in a man who never really deserved it.

There was something between us that was stronger than attraction, infatuation, lust, love or hate. It was as if fate had placed us together to walk a journey that no human power could have prevented. We would continue to see each other, exclusively at first, then in and out of other relationships and then back together.

Paul started to pick me up at least four times a week for dinner and sex. I eventually just wanted the sex and started driving to his apartment myself. It was about five weeks into this relationship that Paul started introducing me to some new ideas about sex; which wasn't difficult as I had always been a willing student. I don't think I ever loved Paul; what we had was an addiction. An addiction to each other and the power of our sex.

The first thing he introduced me to was the vibrator. He bought one for me and showed me how to use it. I was hooked from the very first powerful orgasm. It was so wonderful I started using it all the time, when I was with him and when I was away from him. I would even use it in my car sometimes as I was driving to work. The orgasm reached with the vibrator was realms above plain masturbation and I loved it.

Then there were the mood altering substances. Up until I met Paul I had only drunk alcohol and smoked pot. Paul used other drugs and found much pleasure in introducing me to them. Hash oil, PCP, ups, downs, acid, cocaine – we did them all. I enjoyed using them, mixed with the intense sex, I was hooked. My life had become and endless blur of days at work and nights filled with Paul and his friends, drinking, drugging, and sex.

I was consumed by the sex and I was swept away by my new life. This was a life that felt free. Free to be myself, free to feel pleasure, free to enjoy all that life had to offer and with Paul it seemed as if it offered a lot. He was good to me in many ways and had always spoiled me. He bought me beautiful clothes, took me to exclusive clubs, took me on trips to places we could play our sex games. It was a fascinating and beautiful partnership.

One night he decided it was time to introduce me to what I was to learn was his favorite fetish. He found intense pleasure in the game of sado-masochism. He wanted me to make him my slave. At times, when I had a sufficient amount of mood altering chemicals in my system I would have no trouble being the dominant, but I longed to be on the submissive side. I begged him to tie me up; I would tell him how I could be better if he let me experience the other side. One night after we had been out dancing and drinking quite heavily he gave in to my wishes. He tied me to the black leather chair and whet my appetite by smacking the riding crop on the bed. With each hit I could feel the excitement explode inside of me. Then, when I least expected it, he brought the riding crop across my ass so hard I saw stars. Before the pain left he struck me again, and again. I screamed. I cried. I was hooked. He stopped. He untied me and my body crumbled to the floor. I laid there in my pain for what seemed like hours. Paul went to sleep in the bed leaving me on the floor.

I listened to Paul's breathing wondering how he could sleep, and then I heard the door open and Phillip came into the room and lifted me gently into his arms holding me close to his naked body. He carried me into his bed and made sweet love to me. Phillip was so gentle, but the other pain lingered and made it feel so passionate. That would be the one and only time Phillip would ever have sex with me, and it left a powerful memory.

Chapter 4

Paul and I had entered a period in our relationship where others were coming and going through our lives. Paul had decided to see other women and I had started dating one of his friends. Michael was a stock broker and quite a story teller. I was entertained. He was around thirty eight and I was now twenty one. He had the most amazing imagination and he constantly fascinated me with his playful antics. We had a lot of fun together but mostly we had a lot of sex. He was quite talented and he taught me a lot about pleasure. Being with him was always a wonderful experience.

Michael lived in a loft apartment in the center of the city. It was a short distance from my work and most nights we would meet for drinks and dinner and then we would walk to his place for a night of sex.

There was an Italian restaurant we loved to go to, Vincent's. The food was amazing; especially the artichokes. We would order two, sit real close and feed each other. I would pick off a leaf, dip it in the melted butter that would drip down my fingers and raise it to Michael's mouth. He would suck the tender flesh off the tip, making delicious sounds. He would do the same for me and after several minutes our passion would explode. I would beg him to come to the ladies' room with me. It was always exciting.

The ladies' room in Vincent's was small but it had this large porcelain sink that Michael would rest me against as he pumped into me until we both had intense orgasms. The cool porcelain always felt wonderful as I would fall forward touching it with my breasts and then Michael would pull me back into him. It was intoxicating to me and the fear of getting discovered always added to the excitement.

After a few months we started taking our sex to new places in search of new exhilaration. We both liked to play games in public. No place was too risky for us. The pleasure would just build and build with each new adventure. One of our favorite games was "whore in the museum". I would dress up – short skirt, black stockings, garter, no panties, see through blouse over a black lace bra, red lipstick and high heels. We would act as though we didn't know each other and I would get close to him and tease him, tantalize him by touching myself and licking my fingers trying to convince him without words to take me home with him. Most museum people were horrified by my behavior but every once in a while, to our amazement, there would be someone else willing to get in on the game and wish to take me home. Michael would give up some nights for fun, but he never let me go home with the other man.

I know it wasn't love with me and Michael, it was lust. Just flesh, addiction to pleasure; and with any addiction there was always the need for more. More pleasure, more excitement, more fun, more danger. I had reached a point with Michael where I needed him to feel alive, whole, complete. I would do anything for him including throwing my soul away.

Michael took me shopping one Saturday and bought me a beautiful ankle length black dress that flowed smoothly on my small frame. That night he invited me to join him at a party wearing my new black dress. The small group of twelve people attending the party were strangers to both Michael and I except for the hostess, Jane, who worked with Michael.

Jane was a beautiful tall blonde. She was wearing a long white dress which was stunning against her honey colored skin. She greeted us both with a warm smile and then handed me the joint she was puffing on. Michael kissed her softly on her bright red lips; I took a long deep drag off the joint. He then turned towards me and sucked the smoke from my mouth as he squeezed my ass. We giggled and headed to the bar.

I had my usual three shots, tonight it was tequila, with an ice water back and Michael had a scotch and soda. We wandered into the room where there were people talking, laughing, eating, drinking and having sex. I scanned the room for someone, anyone, who would be the one, the one I would try first. Michael had gone off in a different direction and I was standing there, feeling shy, a little afraid, not knowing what to do next, but the tequila started to kick in and I got that wonderful warm sensation and my head felt light. Suddenly I felt a gentle hand lift my long hair and then soft lips kissed my neck. This always made my nipples hard and my knees weak. I turned slowly to find myself in the arms of an attractive man. He had on a black silk robe that was open in the front exposing his smooth tanned body. He carefully lifted my dress over my head and laid it over the back of a nearby chair. He sat on the chair and pulled me down on him. The immediate sensation took my breath away and then we got into a rhythmic motion which made me orgasm is a very short time.

Michael and I attended many more of those parties and most of them were fun, I always found pleasure with one or more during an evening. Michael enjoyed it, too. He loved to have sex with me later, telling me about the other women in great detail.

One evening we went to a party in the suburbs. We did not know the host or hostess. We had been invited by a woman Michael had met at an earlier party. There was something about this party that was different, not as upscale as the ones we usually attended in the city. I was off that night myself and not really getting into anyone but Michael seemed to be enjoying himself. I was in an observing mode – watching the other people having sex when I came across this fat woman and her poodle. She had trained the poodle to lick her until she had an orgasm and she was trying to convince me to try it. This is where I had to draw the line. I ended up locking myself in the bathroom with a gram of cocaine and a bottle of gin that night and that was the end of our orgy experiment.

After a short while, we started going down to the red light district. The element of sleaziness added to the excitement for both of us. We would watch the shows and have sex with each other as we talked about the people in the show; feeling the passion of sharing our flesh with the imaginary others. Knowing that at any moment we were both capable of actually sharing our flesh.

We would go to strip bars and watch the beautiful women move their hips, touch their breasts exposing their luscious young bodies inches away from us. We would whisper stories to each other as we watched them and we would tell stories again later that night in bed. Our need for creativity grew and my hunger was insatiable. I became more detached from my body. I increasingly found pleasure in the imaginings of Michael's mind.

It was intoxicating.

I was hooked.

I was starting to lose touch with reality and the drinking, drugging and intense sex, were all taking their toll on me.

Chapter 5

Michael refused to get into the bondage thing, so Paul and I would still see each other occasionally to engage in that activity together. Michael didn't mind and in spite of the fact that he did not want to inflict them, he found my bruises and rope burns exciting. He enjoyed hearing me talk about it while we had sex. Michael loved to hear how I felt as I was tied to the bed, helpless, unable to escape the punishment being inflicted on me and he also found excitement in the vivid descriptions of what Paul felt like as he wielded his power over me and took what he wanted and doled out pain.

This combination was extraordinary to all of us. Paul enjoyed knowing that he played a part in my tantalizing fantasies when he was with me and when he was away from me. The sex with Michael was incredible and my need to see Paul more frequently consumed me. I was inebriated by our dangerous game. After a while though, the dangerous game seeped into every part of my life and it all started to blur. I was having trouble showing up for work, my mind was only filled with thoughts of bondage games with Paul and creating fantasies for Michael. It was getting increasingly sick and we loved it.

The bondage games were so intense at times that I could not get out of bed for a couple of days after. Michael would have to come and get me at Paul's and sometimes we would just have sex there. This activity seemed strange even to me, but we had lost the choice of whether or not we would have sex. It was just convenient to do it in Paul's bed. I was now wearing blue jeans and long sleeve shirts all the time to cover the bruises and rope burns the bondage games left on my body and I was drinking all the time. When I was with Paul I got high on Quaaludes and when I was with Michael we used cocaine and marijuana. I hardly ever went out in public with either of them anymore, I was such a mess.

I can't even remember how much time had passed. Each day blurred into night and each night melted into day. I was usually at either Michael's or Paul's. They were both tiring of my drinking, drugging and sick behavior. It was not long before each of them kicked me out.

I was lost without them.

My dependency on their attention and games was so powerful I thought I would die without them. They both refused to see me until I got myself together, which seemed an impossible task at that time. I was on a downward spiral and I had lost the ability to control or stop it.

I had no job and no place to live as I had lost my apartment due to the fact that I had no income. My friends were finished with my sick behavior and I had abandoned my family so they had abandoned me. I was too screwed up to work and I couldn't pull myself together, the fear and loneliness filled me and oblivion was my only comfort. I needed to use and I owed my dealer a lot of money. He saw this as an opportunity and took me in, and I threw myself away a little more.

Chapter 6

Ray was a tall black man in his mid-twenties. He had been dealing cocaine and marijuana to us for the past couple of years and I never really saw him in a sexual way. Ray, on the other hand, saw my misfortune as an opportunity for me to make good on the debts I owed him. He liked it rough, and I had no choice but to pay up. He would keep me high and I would keep him satisfied. This lasted for a while till he got bored with the mess that I had become. Then I had just become a possession Ray would use when he needed to.

Ray's business had been getting bigger and one night he met with two Columbians to do a really big deal. As usual Ray cleaned me up and dragged me along. One of them acted as though he liked me, and Ray just gave me to him. He took me back to his hotel room, tied me to the bed and raped and sodomized me for the rest of the night. In the morning I could hardly walk and he put me in a cab and sent me back to Ray. This incident showed me what I had become and it also showed Ray what kind of people he was dealing with. Ray never let on but I knew he got the message.

Ray wasn't always a bad guy. He had his moments of humanity and kindness; he even helped me get straightened out and healthy. This was only because he saw it as a chance to pay him back in a new way. Ray knew I was smart and good looking and he decided to take advantage of that. I was no longer a liability. I had become a great asset.

Chapter 7

I had developed a relationship with Paul's lawyer who would pay dearly for discreet marijuana and cocaine deals. I became his dealer but only if I stayed clean around him. I agreed to keep it together and once a week I would visit Abe at his office. He was a very interesting character and a very successful lawyer. His office was in the city overlooking the park and I found peace just being there. We became friends and he actually looked forward to seeing me. Sometimes he would take me to lunch and other times we would just sit in his office together have coffee quietly watching people in the park. It was strange that a man like him would become an anchor in my life. He was a good friend and I owed him a lot for this friendship.

Abe wanted to help me get paid up with Ray but Ray wasn't going to let me go that easy. He had become accustomed to using me and he needed me. Business was getting bigger and he liked the way I was always able to negotiate the best deals for him with the Columbians. Most of them really liked me and they let Ray get away with stuff just so they could spend more time with me. I had been able to keep myself relatively clean, I was still drinking, but I had stopped using cocaine and I only occasionally smoked pot with Abe. I was able to control what happened with the Columbians so I had not been hurt again. Ray never protected me, only his interest in the cash he was making by his partnerships with the Columbians. I never really trusted them and there was always something going on just under the surface.

One night something went wrong, really wrong. Ray was making a big deal and he wanted me there to keep everyone calm and happy. I had been drinking a little that evening but I was on top of things. Ray had a few lines before we left to meet the Columbians at their hotel but he was okay, too. We had been laughing at some jokes as we entered the lobby of the hotel, a cheap flophouse. I had not noticed the two men in suits by the front desk as we strolled towards the elevator carrying the aluminum brief case that contained the money for the deal.

I was wearing a short skirt, fish net hose, heels, a tight sweater and my blonde wig. We actually looked like a hooker and her pimp, which, in this part of town didn't really get anyone's attention; but the aluminum briefcase did.

We stepped on the elevator and so did the two men in suits. They didn't say anything to us but we knew something was up. So I climbed all over Ray calling "baby" trying to explain to him why I didn't have more cash for him. The elevator ride to the fifth floor seemed like it took minutes instead of seconds. We were busy making out when the elevator stopped and the doors opened. No one got out. One of the men finally said, "Isn't this your floor?" We looked at each other and Ray said, "oh yeah, thanks man" and we got off. They did not follow us off the elevator; I had a moment of relief, which was instantly replaced with a very uncomfortable feeling.

I don't think Ray had the same feelings that I did. I was scared. I was not sure if my uneasy feelings were about the Columbians or that maybe the suits were FBI. I just knew I wanted to take an immediate detour to the room. I saw the door to the bathroom and told Ray that I would catch up with him as I ducked in. I locked the door behind me and tried to think what I was going to do next to get out of this. I suddenly felt quite sober.

I looked at myself in the mirror and knew that I was not going down with Ray this way. I scanned the room for an exit. Fortunately I was in a sleazy old hotel in the red light district and the window opened to a fire escape. I slid it open and climbed up on the ledge. I was able to reach the fire escape and make my way only to the next level down. I was hanging there not knowing what to do next when I saw the glow of a cigarette in the dark balcony to my left. I froze for a moment not knowing who was standing there watching me on the fire escape. I am sure I was quite a sight. I looked down, I wasn't going that way, I looked up, there was no real escape that way either.

Ray would be wondering what happened to me by now and I knew he would be trying to get into the bathroom any minute. I quietly called to the person smoking in the dark on the balcony and he walked over into the dim light. He was a small thin man about forty. He asked if I was all right, although I knew he was not sincere. He had to know that something was strange about a woman hanging on to a fire escape in the middle of the night. I had a sense of relief when I realized he was really unaware as to why I was there on the fire escape, which meant he was just an innocent bystander.

He tossed his cigarette with a flick of his wrist and it fell to the ground in the alley below. He reached for my hand and pulled me on to the balcony. Without a word he then took my hand and led me into his room. I was afraid and needed a moment to figure out how I was going to get out of this. I felt cornered. What was happening to Ray, the Columbians, if they were Columbians, the Feds? It seemed too quiet. I tried to listen, to hear just the slightest clue as to what was happening. Then all hell broke loose, I heard a shot from the floor above and lots of heavy footsteps. I decided to toss one of my heels and my blonde wig into the alley to make it look like I ran.

My pulse was racing and I was having trouble deciding how to play out the next move. I did not really want to involve my new savior but I no choice, he was in it. It would just be a matter of time now that they would start a room to room search for me. I wasn't sure if they would believe that I had run. This looked like a good time to introduce myself and explain briefly that I desperately needed his help.

Roger, that was his name. Sales. Not going very well these days which explained this hotel. I looked in his closet and decided I had only one shot at pulling this off. I asked Roger to strip out of his clothes and put on his robe which was hanging in the closet next to two suits, a pair of jeans, and two sport shirts. I tossed the pants and white shirt on the floor by the bed and also the jeans and one of the sport shirts. I went to the sink and wet my hair and pulled it tightly into a ponytail. I stripped and hid my clothes in the closet. I got into his bed and positioned myself. It wasn't long until we heard the knock on the door.

Roger looked at me with panic and excitement in his eyes. I told him it would be okay and to take his time getting to the door. I pulled the covers up around me and Roger opened the door until the chain stopped it. Male voices asked him if he had seen a woman, small blonde. Roger replied that he had not, and indicated he was not alone. The cop looked over at the bed and then observing the two pairs of men's clothes on the floor decided Roger was engaging in behavior they wanted no part of. They mumbled that they were sorry; Roger looked so innocent and ashamed at being found out. He closed the door.

I couldn't believe it worked. Roger had a sense of relief on his face but mostly he was excited. His heart was pumping out adrenaline and his brain was drunk with his new found excitement. He jumped on the bed like a playful boy who had just gotten away with some sort of immoral sin. I sat up and the sheet fell away from my chest exposing my small breasts and started to laugh. Roger stared at my chest and then paused for a moment. Then he reached out and cupped my breasts in his hands. I was surprised to find out that

I was also very excited. He pushed me back on the bed with a force I would not have expected and then started kissing me, my mouth, my neck, my arms, my stomach, my thighs, my knees, oh my!

I don't know how long it had been for Roger but he was sure enjoying his new found strength and excitement. I think he felt like a hero, that he had somehow saved the damsel in distress. What a stud. We had sex for a long time, only stopping when exhaustion and sleep had finally taken over.

I knew I could not stay there and that I would have to get out of the hotel somehow, there were still cops and Feds everywhere. This must have been quite a bust for them. Thankfully Roger was a small guy and I was able to borrow something from him to disguise myself enough to get out of there. I left him lying on the bed in his crappy room in his skid row hotel with a very big smile on his sweet face. I knew he would think of this night often and that made me smile. Being the center of someone's thoughts was always mesmeric for me.

I did make it out of the hotel without incident and managed to hail a cab a few blocks away. I immediately went to Abe's office. I could not go home and I had no idea what had happened to Ray. There were things I needed to know and Abe was the one person who could get answers.

I was a bit jittery while waiting for his receptionist to announce me. I didn't have very much sleep but most of all it had been quite a few hours since I had anything to drink or smoke. At the very least I needed coffee. Abe greeted me warmly and asked the receptionist to bring us some coffee as he directed me into his office. He sat next to me on the sofa and asked if I was all right and to explain to him everything that happened the night before. But most of all, I could see in his eyes that he wanted to know if anyone else knew where I was right now. I don't blame Abe for wanting to protect himself, he had a lot to protect, least of which was me. He did protect me. I felt safe when I was with him; the thing I did not know at that time was that Abe walked a dangerous line in his life as well. I told him everything, including the part about Roger. A sense of relief washed over his face when he realized that they never did make a connection as to who I was to Ray. Then he told me that Ray had been shot and killed by the FBI agents in the hotel last night.

Chapter 8

Abe was like an angel that day. He called Sheila, his girlfriend, and asked her to take me shopping and then take me to his home; he knew that I could not go back to Ray's and that everything I had there was lost.

Sheila was a beautiful woman. She had long dark hair which fell like silk on her shoulders, I imagined Abe burying his face in her hair. She was tall and thin and had one of those beautiful smiles that would light up a dark room, with a dimple on her left cheek. Her eyes, hazel, sparkled with life. She took me to her favorite boutique and taught me about dressing with class. She selected things that were elegant but showed off my thin body. I felt beautiful, sexy. We told each other stories and laughed, she had a wonderful way of taking your mind off your troubles, and I knew why Abe loved her. I started to love her that day.

When we got back to Abe's house Sheila asked Bridgett the housekeeper to show me to the guest house and help me get settled in. Bridgett was a small round French woman who had been working for Abe for the last five years. She was very nice and had a wonderful laugh, a contagious laugh.

The guest house was just off the end of the pool deck, north of the main house. There were two steps up to a small porch with French doors opening into the living room. The décor was simple; wood flooring, brown leather couch and matching love seat, Oriental rug on the floor between them with a glass coffee table on it. There were fresh flowers in a crystal vase on the coffee table along with a crystal cigarette box and crystal ashtray. We walked through the living room into the bedroom which had a beautiful four poster bed with a soft cream bedspread and lots of beautiful pillows. There was a dresser and a small table on each side of the bed. The lighting was subtle track lighting mounted near the ceiling over the bed. There was a small vase of whisper pink sweetheart roses on the dresser.

Bridgett hung up my new wardrobe and drew a bath for me. Then she left the room.

As I slipped out of my clothes I watched myself in the mirror and I was reminded of the innocence I once possessed. An innocence that had slipped away or maybe it had been torn away. I climbed gingerly into the beautiful marble tub; the water was warm and very comforting. The bubble bath Bridgett put into the water smelled of gardenias which filled the whole room. I felt relaxed and I closed my eyes and started reflecting on all the happenings of the last twenty-four hours. I felt like I could sleep forever. Just then Sheila walked in and handed me a joint and a glass of white wine. She sat on the edge of the tub and asked how I was doing. I loved her tenderness and I felt safe with her there. We smoked the joint and sipped the wine and laughed.

I was warming up the water in the tub when Abe appeared at the door with a big smile on his face. Sheila got up immediately and went to him, he grabbed her around her thin waist leaned her back and gave her a wonderfully passionate kiss. The kind of kiss most women only dream of getting. The sight of that kiss made me reach between my legs and rub my clitoris. My head fell back and pleasure filled my body. They were so busy with each other that I was sure they had not noticed. Abe then took Sheila by the hand and led her away.

A few minutes later Bridgett appeared and helped me out of the bath and told me that dinner would be served at seven. As I dried myself I glanced around the room, which was white marble from floor to ceiling. The countertop which was the full width of the room and was also marble, with mirrors covering the entire wall behind it.

When I walked back into the bedroom I noticed that Sheila had laid out the emerald green silk slip dress and black ankle strap heels. I smiled.

It was six fifteen already so I did not have time to rest. I had to get ready.

I stood in front of the mirror and let the towel drop to the floor. Even though it was summer my skin had not taken on that bronze glow. I could not remember the last time I just got outside to enjoy the sunshine. I pulled back my shoulder length red hair into a ponytail, letting some of the curls fall around my face. Sheila had left some blush, mascara, and lipstick in the drawer for me. I did not have to use more than that. She had chosen the perfect color blush, it reminded me of the Painted Desert, and I brushed it lightly over my ivory skin. I carefully applied the fire engine red lipstick and as I brought the tissue I used to blot the lipstick away from my mouth and looked at myself in the mirror I saw that the color was perfect. My face had taken on a beautiful radiance.

I put lotion on my legs with long strokes rubbing it in and feeling the firmness of my muscles massaging it up between my thighs and across my abdomen. I took a moment to smooth out the short red hair with my fingers. I put more lotion in my hand and applied it to my stomach running my hands over my small hips and round ass.

I was sure Sheila had chosen all the toiletries for this bathroom, everything smelled delicious, just like her. I paused to think about how beautiful she is and how good she smelled. Abe was a lucky guy to have her in his life. I applied lotion to my breasts rubbing them with circular motions squeezing my nipples between my fingers. This felt good and my thoughts turned provocative. I imagined rubbing lotion on Sheila's beautiful breasts, her olive skin, flat stomach, long legs. I was mesmerized and still massaging my breasts when I heard a knock and Abe's voice beckoned me to join them on the patio.

I walked over to the bed and picked up the delicate dress slipped it over my head and felt the delicious softness of the silk fall over my body. I stepped into the shoes and bent down to buckle the thin straps around my ankles. As I stood up I caught my reflection in the full length mirror next to the bed and felt satisfied at how beautiful I looked. The green of the dress made my green eyes greener. I strolled out of the room towards the patio with a confident stride.

Out on the patio Abe and Sheila were laughing and sipping on what looked like margaritas. Abe greeted me with a soft kiss on my fire engine red lips and Sheila gave me a hug with a gentle kiss on my cheek. Her touch gave me a warm feeling of excitement. "You look stunning my dear" came from her full red lips, a mouth so beautiful, so delicious, it made me blush. I told her it was her fault and she smiled that smile that could light up a room.

Abe was standing there handing me this big icy green drink, I looked at it and then with apology in my voice said "no thanks." I walked over to the bar and reached for the bottle of Jack Daniels and poured a double into a crystal rocks glass and drank it down in one gulp. As I picked up the bottle to pour another I felt the warmth of the shot explode in my stomach sending heat up into my chest, down my arms and legs into my toes and finger tips. I loved that feeling. It was the best. Abe just shook his head and smiled, he knew that I was on my way to la la land, he had seen it before. His expression surprised me and I felt a little shame, I decided to hold off on the second double for now.

Abe put on some salsa music and the Latin beat made my hips start to sway, the drink had gone to my head a little and I started to snap my fingers and move my feet to the sexy beat. Sheila joined me and we both started to dance around Abe. He was enjoying the show. Sheila moved her body to the beat, lifting her arms up and clapping her hands over her head like a Spanish Flamenco dancer. I imitated her and we both started laughing. We grabbed each others hands and she spun me around, the music went into a Tango and Sheila pulled me close to her, chest to chest and started to lead me in a Tango. This is a beautiful dance, a very sexy passionate dance; I felt the ecstasy well up inside me. Abe felt it too. He watched us. Sheila's hair brushed against my cheek, I smelled her sweetness, I felt her softness. My heart was racing, my knees were weak, just then Abe broke in and finished the dance with Sheila. I just stood and watched. I felt jealous. Their bodies moved in perfect synchronicity together, it was so sexy watching them, cheek to cheek, legs touching, bodies touching, I felt a quiver between my thighs and let out a whimper of excitement. Just as I started to lose my balance, I felt a hand on my back and a moist kiss on my neck; it startled and excited me and when I looked up I saw Paul's eyes. Eyes that I missed. A touch that I missed. A mouth that I missed.

Paul pulled the clip from my hair and my red curls fell down onto my shoulders. He pulled me into him holding my wrists behind my back. The heat in my body rose and I surrendered to his passion, his mouth pressed hard against mine. I felt the wetness between my legs and the sexual urges rose from deep inside me. I lifted my right leg up and wrapped it over his hip. It had been so long since I felt his touch, his mouth, his passion. Was it true, was it possible, was I really pressed against him. The excitement felt good. Paul felt good. He lifted me off the ground and carried me into the cabana. Once inside he set me down on the countertop pushed my legs apart and knelt down in front of me and started to pleasure me with his tongue. I squealed with pleasure. He loved that he could still please me. "I have missed your sweetness," is all he said as he continued to pleasure me. I could feel the warm of his mouth and the stiffness of his tongue moving in and out bringing so much pleasure. I could not wait any longer, I screamed, my body shook and shuddered. Paul stood up held me close and put his tongue in my mouth and down my throat.

I loved his passion. I missed his passion. He released his grip and my body fell back against the wall relaxed but not satiated.

Chapter 9

I missed Paul for so many reasons but the thing I missed most about him was the feeling of being desired. He had a wonderful way of making me feel beautiful. I think this is what I wanted most from him. The idea that I was the one he wanted more than anything in the world. This is what my addiction to him was about. I burned for him because I felt he desired me. I needed this as I needed air to breathe. Tonight was no different; there he was in front of me giving me this gift, the gift of desirability. The gift I needed most, the gift that fed my soul; or so I thought.

Abe and I really never talked about Paul. Maybe Paul talked about me. I don't know what brought him to Abe's that night but I was so glad he came. Bridgett announced dinner and the four of us moved towards the table on the south end of the patio. As with all the furnishings in Abe's home the patio table was the most elegant I had ever seen. Bridgett had set the table beautifully; candles, linen napkins, china, crystal and silver. Paul pulled a chair out for me and I sat on the edge as he moved it gently forward. He sat next to me. Sheila sat down across from me and shot me a look which made me giggle with a little guilt. Abe was busy lifting a bottle of champagne from the ice bucket set up next to the table. I loved champagne and was excited to see it. I loved the way the bubbles tickled my nose and how it felt so refreshing as it slipped past my tongue and down my throat but I most loved the way it made my head feel, light and very sexy.

I reminded myself to take it easy and Abe also reminded me with a gentle squeeze to my shoulder as he set a glass in front of me. I think Abe really loved me and wanted the best for me. He was a wonderful friend. I never wanted to let him down, but I did so many times. When everyone had a glass in their hand

31

Paul made a toast to friends, we all cheered. They sipped the champagne while I swallowed the entire contents of my glass in one gulp.

Dinner was fabulous although I did not eat very much. My mind kept drifting to sex with Paul. By the time cognac was served, Paul had his hand on my thigh and I felt the wetness between my legs. Abe was watching Paul's hand through the glass top table and leaned towards Sheila and whispered something in her ear. She blushed and then they both excused themselves from the table. Paul stood up as Sheila rose; she smiled and blew a kiss to him across the table. Abe said nothing as he lifted their two cognacs from the table and disappeared with them and Sheila.

Paul pulled my chair away from the table and sat back down. I remained in my chair waiting for Paul to take the lead. I so wanted him, I so wanted him to want me. My head felt light and I was feeling playful. We sat there in silence for a few moments and then Paul reached for my hand pulling me on to his lap. "You look so beautiful, I have missed you." "I have missed you too," is all I could say as I dropped my head on to his shoulder. He felt good, he smelled good. I wanted him so much at that moment. I felt incredibly gentle and so did he. We sat there holding each other for a while then he stood up forcing me to my feet. He lifted me up and carried me across the pool deck towards the guest house. As we passed the bar, I grabbed the bottle of Jack.

Once inside, he dropped me onto the leather couch I was still holding the Jack. The leather felt cool against my bare legs and I could smell the fragrance of the flowers in the vase on the coffee table. Paul then put two shot glasses down on the coffee table, took the Jack from my grasp and poured us each a shot. I threw my head back and swallowed and so did he. I reached for the bottle again but this time I just raised it to my mouth. The warmth of the whiskey exploded in my chest. My head was light; I fell back on the couch to enjoy this wonderful intoxication.

Paul sat next to me and pulled my legs up into his lap. He put his hand under my left foot and raised it to his mouth. He ran his tongue between each of my toes, which always tickled me, and I let out a giggle. He continued running his tongue across the top of my foot stopping at my ankle. He moved the ankle strap aside slightly and stared as if to see the scars from the burns he had left there in the past. This made my heart skip and I could feel the excitement building inside. He watched my face as he moved his hand up my leg and slid his fingers into my wet vagina. My body jerked, my mouth opened and a delicious sound emerged. He covered my mouth with his and put his tongue down my throat. I was so excited I came right then. As my body quivered and jerked with this excitement, Paul removed his pants and mounted me. It was divine; more divine than I had remembered. It felt good. He felt good. We had sex for a while on the couch and then moved into the bed. Of course I brought the Jack along not knowing when I would get thirsty again. The sex was wonderful but I eventually passed out. When I woke up the next day Paul was gone, the bed was tossed and the bottle was empty. We must have had fun.

I wondered where Paul had gone, why had he left me, was he coming back. I needed him already.

I staggered to the bathroom, mascara was smudged below my eyes, my hair was tangled. I looked frightful. I really needed to stop drinking so much I thought as my head pounded with each step. I peed, then stepped into the shower. The warm water felt good running over my hair and down my back. I closed my eyes and thought about Paul, his touch, his body next to mine.

I missed him already. Where had he gone?

I got out of the shower wrapped a towel around my head and slipped my wet body into the terry robe that was hanging on the hook. I walked slowly and deliberately out to the pool deck to see if anyone else was around. Sheila was sitting at the table having a cup of coffee and reading the paper. I sat down across from her. She looked up and smiled, "Did you sleep well my dear?" She said and she didn't even wait for my response before her eyes fell back onto the paper. I just sat there, silent. Bridgett appeared with a cup of coffee for me and a tall glass of orange juice which she placed carefully in front of me. It was already warm although it was only slightly after 9:00 am. I pulled the towel off my head and loosened my robe. "Where is Abe? Where is Paul?" I asked Sheila. She looked up and said "Abe's at the office, and I wasn't sleeping with Paul so I don't know where he is" and then she laughed. This made me laugh, too.

I drank the coffee and decided the pool looked inviting, I stood up, dropped the robe and dove in the deep end, which was symbolic of my life. I always dove into the deep end. As I swam the length of the pool, I could think of nothing but Paul. I wanted him to return, I wanted to know why he left. We had not really talked to each other so I had no idea if he intended to return. I just knew I needed him. I swam a total of five laps. Nearly exhausted, I had a hard time pulling myself up the ladder back onto the pool deck. Sheila was still reading the paper. The sun was glistening off her dark hair and her mouth was wrapped around a piece of melon, she looked beautiful. I loved her. I picked up the robe and towel and strolled back to the guest house without a word.

Chapter 10

The weeks dragged by. I was moody and restless. I did not hear a word from Paul and I could not keep myself from thinking about him and how much I needed his attention. Sheila tried to keep me busy. She was a part time photographer for a small glossy publication and took me on a couple of photo shoots. It was fun, interesting and to my delight I met some intelligent and fascinating people.

Sheila and I dined at wonderful restaurants and she took me to a few cocktail parties. I learned about so many new things. Sheila was teaching me about art and culture in a way I had not experienced them in my life. I was educated, went to college, but had not seen the world Sheila lived in before now. I really liked it, but I often felt like a fraud. I would just stand back and watch her friends interact with each other; talking of art and books, artists and writers – things I knew little about but I was learning. Mostly I loved being with Sheila. Sometimes we would take long walks and she would tell me stories of beautiful places she had visited and wonderful people she had met. Sometimes we would lie in the sun by the pool and she would give me books to read, most of which I enjoyed.

I was blessed to have Sheila, Abe and Bridgett in my life.

Chapter 11

I had managed to remain reasonable around my alcohol and drug usage out of respect for Abe and Sheila. They were so good to me. Not only did they give me a place to stay but they made sure I ate, got exercise, and felt loved. Even though I had all this from Abe and Sheila it was getting increasingly hard not to return to the emotional place that felt familiar the emotional place that was about throwing myself away. Feelings deep inside that enabled me to stay with Ray, feelings that enabled me to be with Paul and Michael. I missed the excitement. Most of all I missed Paul. I was strangely addicted to him. I knew I just threw myself away bit by bit with Paul but I just could not stop wanting him, his attention, his sex. He had not come back to see me in all these weeks. Did he not know that I desperately needed him? Why had he not come back, why had he come that first night?

It was a beautiful summer evening and I was sitting by the pool smoking a joint and sipping on some whiskey when Sheila and Abe sat down to join me. It had actually been a while since Abe and I had one of our long deep talks. Everything seemed so different in my life now. I felt more lonely and yet more loved than I had in a long time. It must have been the physical connection that I was craving, the one place I could find sanctuary, sex. Sex had always been a distraction for me, something that would help me forget everything else and make me feel connected to another human being; even though it was always brief.

Sex was intoxicating.

Abe loved me, but he knew he wasn't doing me a favor by taking care of me. He knew it was time for me to get back on my feet and move forward in my life. I knew it too. I was now twenty three and I needed to grow up a little more. I told Abe I was ready to get back to work and take care of myself. "I love you" was his only response. I drank the rest of my double Jack and decided to go to the club and have some fun. Abe and Sheila declined the invitation to join me, so I decided to go alone. It had been a while since I had been to the club, but there would be people I knew there. I would have fun.

Sheila, Abe and I had dinner that night on the patio. Bridgett had once again created a wonderful meal for us. After dinner I excused myself from the table and went to the guest house to get ready to go out. Abe and Sheila moved into the living room to read. I saw them through the window sitting together on the couch, touching, being one, yet separate. I envied them. They were in love with each other. I did not have any idea how to love and I wasn't very good at being loved, either.

On the way to the guest house I had snatched a bottle of gin from the bar along with a crystal rocks glass. Once inside the guest house I placed the glass on the marble counter in the bathroom and poured myself a double, which I drank down in one gulp.

I slipped out of my dress and got into the shower. The warm water felt good, my head started to feel light. My skin had finally taken on the bronze glow from the sun and I looked good. I decided to wear a simple black dress and my black ankle strap heels. I let my red curls fall over my shoulders and I only needed some lipstick to complete the job. I had a couple more doubles during the process and I was feeling a bit light headed by the time the cab arrived.

The cab driver was a nice looking young man with a sparkle in his eyes, he chatted to me all the way to the club, but I had not really heard anything he said. I was distracted by thoughts of Paul. Would he be there, would I see him tonight? I could only hope so.

Once in front of the club, I gave the driver a ten and told him to keep the change. He thanked me and helped me out of the cab. As I approached the front door of the club Raleigh, the owner, greeted me with a big hug and asked where I had been. "Trying to stay clean" is all I replied and we both laughed.

Raleigh was a good looking man. He had a warm way with people and knew how to have fun. He had a wife, two teenage children and a beautiful mistress named Precious. Precious was at the club most nights. I guess his wife didn't care as long as she had what she needed from him and that was a lot.

I strolled inside and immediately went to the bar to order my usual shot straight up with an ice water back; tonight it was gin. Pete was bartending tonight and he blew me a kiss as he put the glasses down on the bar. I drank the shot, slammed the glass on the bar, winked at Pete, picked up the ice water and wandered towards the dance floor.

My favorite band, Spin, was finishing up the last song in the set. I stood at the edge of the dance floor, closed my eyes and moved my hips to the tune they were playing. It felt good to be at the club, excitement filled the air. The music stopped abruptly and then the DJ put on some disco tune.

Steve, the lead singer, grabbed me and lifted me off the floor as he spun me around like a child. "Haven't seen you for a while, you look great, let's go grab a smoke" he said as he pulled me towards the back door. Once outside he lit up a joint and handed me a Quaalude. "Have a party baby!"

I tossed the Quaalude in my mouth and grabbed his drink to wash it down. "Yuk, what are you drinking?" I asked, my face twisted from the odd taste. "Shirley Temple or course" he said with a seriousness that made us both laugh out loud. We chatted for a while and finished the joint and then it was time for Steve to get back on stage. I went off to the ladies' room and I was feeling a bit screwed up from the gin, Quaalude, pot and the excitement of the club. I made my way back to the dance floor; it was about midnight and the place was crowded. I stopped along the way to get another shot from Pete and some ice water, as my mouth was dry from the pot.

As I approached the dance floor, a good looking man with long blonde hair and big blue eyes gently held my hand, took my drink and led me on to the dance floor. I was feeling quite free and putting on a delicious show for him. He was enjoying it and so was I. I had always been a bit of an exhibitionist and tonight I was enjoying being the center of his attention. We danced for a while and then the next thing I was aware of was being out in back of the club lying on the hood on a small car with this guy's tongue down my throat and his penis in my vagina. I would have objected, but it felt good. I was so messed up and even though this situation was daring, more daring than even I would usually do, I was incredibly excited by it. I must have slipped back into a blackout because the next thing I was conscious of was being back in the club with Steve giving him a blow job. Before I could figure out where we were, Steve let out a deep throaty moan, yanked his penis from my mouth and ejaculated all over the front of my dress. I was just too messed up to give a damn. I lost my balance and fell over; as I lay there on the floor I finally realized we were in Raleigh's office. Steve tossed me a towel; gave me a shirt to put on over my dress and called me a cab.

Raleigh put me in the cab and sent me back to Abe's. I stumbled all the way across the pool deck, finally making it into the guest house. I did manage to get in the shower and wash off the nights happenings. I felt like shit. It must have been the gin. I needed some sleep.

"No more Quaaludes" I said out loud to no one but myself before I fell across the bed. It wasn't the first time I had gotten that messed up and I knew it wouldn't be the last. What I didn't know at that moment was how many more humiliations I would have to bear because of my addictions.

All the things I thought brought me freedom were the same things that would eventually hold me prisoner. I just could not see it coming. I did not realize that I could not stop being this woman-child I had become.

Chapter 12

I got a job at a woman's clothing store at a shopping mall out in the suburbs. I was hired as assistant manager but within a month they made me manager of the store. I had not done this type of work since I had worked with Jack. I really liked the work and felt as if I had found my place in the working world.

Along with my new job, I was also able to find a small basement apartment nearby. The home was owned by Helga; she was from Germany and had come to America with her husband after the war. He had recently died and she did not like being in the house alone, so she rented out the basement. She was very nice, but very stoic.

It was winter now and the apartment was cool and damp most of the time. The concrete floors were cold but Helga had put beautiful sheepskin area rugs throughout. The bed was an old iron military style she had painted gold. A pink chenille bedspread and lots of little throw pillows made it seem warm and inviting. The sofa was cream brocade and the dresser was a large French provincial style with a big mirror. There was a small kitchen area with a table and two chairs. The tiny bathroom had a pink sink, a white commode and a little pink and white tile shower stall. It was not like living in the guest house at Abe's, but it was home. I managed to bring warmth to the place with candles, incense, a few plants that did not mind the low light and some vases of dried flowers. I had a small television which I did not watch much, a radio which I played low, and a stack of books and magazines next to my bed that I never had time to read.

I usually spent as much as sixty hours a week at the store. Most days, I had a hard time leaving. My work had become my identity.

I had been smoking a little pot and controlling my drinking. I had not dated anyone in a while and I was getting a bit anxious. It seemed like I was controlling everything in my life during this time, even sex.

The only socializing I did was with Max, the manager of this really hip and exciting store that mostly sold blue jeans. I would go down to his shop first thing in the morning and we would sit in his office and smoke a joint and drink coffee. I liked him, but had not engaged in sexual activity with him which was strange for me.

Max was a tall pale man with long brown hair, his right ear was pierced and he had striking blue-gray eyes. He always wore blue jeans and some kind of rock and roll t-shirt. One morning I was having some feelings of loneliness and despair and decided to approach the sex thing. I was in desperate need of physical contact and needed to feel desired. We ended up having a quickie on his desk. This set in motion some of the most basic animal sex I had ever engaged in with a man. We started having sex every chance we got, his office or mine. It was crazy. I was crazy. I could feel the out-of-control feelings taking over but was unable to stop them.

Now and again thoughts of Paul would creep into my mind and make things worse. I knew that I would find other men to fill the hole that Paul had left in my soul; Max was one of them. I knew with Max it was only temporary, though, and most of the time the hole just got bigger and I needed more.

Max was married so the temporary part was more temporary than even I had anticipated. I had to move on, hungry and with a bigger hole in my soul.

Chapter 13

One day on my way to work I met Alberto. He was the cutest thing, long brown curls and big green eyes. He saw me standing at the bus stop and it was cold so he offered me a lift. I climbed into his warm truck and he handed me a joint. We smoked and laughed and he dropped me at the mall. We made no attempt to exchange telephone numbers I knew it was nothing more than what it was, a small distraction.

About a week later, I decided it was time for me to buy myself a car; getting around in the suburbs was more difficult than the city. As I entered the dealership I looked around for someone to help me pick out a car and I spotted Jeff. He was standing by the window and the light was shining on him, causing a white glow around him which added to his angelic features. His hair was honey blonde and pulled back away from his face into a ponytail. His eyes were so big that I could see that they were blue from across the showroom. He was tall, thin, nice ass, and had the most beautiful lips I had ever seen on a man. I froze; he smiled, and I smiled back. He walked slowly towards me, my heart started to beat faster; he touched my hand and my knees went weak. I felt as if he had undressed me and had his way with me even before I could say my name. It was a moment that lasted forever and yet at the same time not long enough.

I did buy a car that day from Jeff and he pressed his card into my hand with his home phone number written on the back as he kissed me gently on my neck and said "Call me." I did.

He picked me up the next evening after work for a ride on his motorcycle. After the ride he took me to his place and we had sex. He was as amazing as he looked. His beautiful lips had caressed me in so many wonderful places and he had the stamina of a long distance runner. I felt so beautiful laying there with him, like I had so many times with Paul. He got up to get us something to drink and I heard him talking to someone and then he appeared at his bedroom door with Alberto, his roommate! We looked at each other and then burst out laughing. Jeff was standing there with a puzzled look on his face.

Alberto reintroduced himself to me and then disappeared; he reappeared a while later with his long brown curls pulled back off his face, no shirt, blue jeans and bare feet holding a joint between his lips and a beer bottle in his hand. Jeff motioned for him to come in and join us. The three of us shared the joint and they told me funny stories and we laughed and laughed. Then Alberto pulled me towards him and kissed me. It felt good, he smelled good, I wanted him, I wanted him to want me. Jeff just watched for a while as Alberto pleasured me with his mouth and I moaned with enjoyment. He gently lifted my legs over his shoulders and penetrated me, at first gently, then rough. This was more than Jeff could stand and he joined in, kissing me then massaging my breasts, I was screaming with pleasure. It seemed like we all came at the same time, the bed actually moved from the vibration of our orgasms. It was an amazing experience and I did not want to stop.

I wanted more.

I was hooked.

Exhausted and temporarily satisfied I lay there with my two new friends in silence smoking another joint. Alberto got us each a beer, which tasted good as the pot had made my mouth so dry. My eyes suddenly caught the time on the clock across the room and I realized I only had a couple of hours before I had to open the store. Against my true desires I got up, put on my clothes and asked if one of them would take me home.   Alberto volunteered handing me a leather jacket. He pulled on a beat up denim jacket over his bare chest and the pair of worn blue jeans he had on earlier along with brown riding boots and led me out to the garage. I yelled goodbye to Jeff who had been laying there motionless for some time.

Once in the garage Alberto fired up his Harley chopper, climbed on and motioned for me to join him. This looked like my kind of motorcycle, very different from the Norton Jeff rode. We screamed through the quiet suburban streets.   I had my arms and legs wrapped around Alberto and I was in heaven as the wind blew my hair back off my face.   I loved this feeling and hoped he would take me for a ride again. He dropped me off in front of Helga's and I tossed his leather to him.   He pulled it on over the denim and took off with a roar down the street; I stood there till I could no longer hear the crack of the V twin engine in the distance.

I did see both Jeff and Alberto again.   The three of us got together at least once a week to engage in very satisfying sex.   It was a bit kinky but I loved it and it always altered my mood.   The sex was great and the drugs were wonderful.   Alberto smoked pot and hash oil, while Jeff used cocaine and Quaaludes. I enjoyed it all. I especially enjoyed them. They both made me the center of attention and I gave them the best sex I could give.   When I was away from them though, I always thought of Paul.

Chapter 14

Paul still had control of me, he still consumed me and I always knew that all he had to do was appear and I would be his. One day he did, he found me, walked right into the store. It was late in the afternoon; the store was quiet, the mall was quiet and he was quiet.

I was on the top landing retrieving the dresses that had been tried on but not purchased from the dressing rooms when I looked down and saw him standing there. My heart stopped! I gasped. Yes he was standing there by the check out counter looking gorgeous, tanned, dark hair pulled back, kissable lips parted slightly, tight faded jeans and denim jacket, looking around the store. It took everything inside of me not to leap off the upper deck into his arms; instead I slowly descended the stairs, gracefully – like Loretta Young.

I was so happy that I was wearing a new dress. It was the kind of dress that made me feel so pretty. The fabric was made of nylon and polyester the kind of material that clings to the body. The bodice was lace and my breasts were subtly exposed. I really loved the way it fell so nicely over my ass and how the handkerchief hem moved elegantly with each step. It was the color of red wine. My lipstick matched the color of the dress and my red hair was pulled up in a twist with a clip holding it in place, small strands framing my face.

His eyes caught my descent when I was halfway down the staircase, then they met mine and his beautiful lips moved into a smile. By the time I reached the bottom of the stairs he had moved to the staircase to meet me. He reached for me, took my face in his hands and gave me a soft romantic kiss. By this time Kim and Brenda were staring at me. I smiled and waved at them and gave into my passions pressing my body fully against him as I gave him a fervent kiss.

I had missed Paul. I had missed his touch, his smell, his mouth. I took his hand and led him back to my office. Once inside I closed the door, he pushed me against it and brought his sweet lips up to my ear, I could feel his warm breath, he whispered "it's only me, no matter how hard you try, it has always been only, me." I wanted to scream that it was a lie but nothing had ever been closer to the truth, yes it was him and only him; we kissed with the urgency of our addiction, licking and biting at each other. I pulled the clip out of my hair and it fell down onto my shoulders, then I pulled off his jacket; mouths never separating, tongues touching, probing. Paul then grabbed me by the hair spun me around leaned me over my desk and lifted my dress up over my ass. He then ran his hands over my ass with the force I enjoyed, the force that I missed, the force which only he understood. I started to moan in anticipation of the pleasure of the pain; the pain only Paul could deliver to me in a most delicious and satisfying way. He loosened his pants, grasped my small hips with vigor and slammed his penis into me, over and over until I screamed in ecstasy. 'Don't stop' is all I could think of. It felt so wonderful. Paul's sex had a way of transforming me to another world; a world of intense pleasure. The pleasure was so powerful that all other things ceased to exist. I had forgotten all about the store, Kim, Brenda, customers. I only existed in one place, under the influence of Paul. My body was pulsating and trembling in his hands. When he released his grip I slumped forward on to the desk knocking the phone off the hook and the desk lamp fell to the floor with a thud. Paul sat down in the chair, big grin of satisfaction on his face. I was in a state of intoxication and I wanted more. I could not look back for fear that he would once again be gone. Fear that he would leave me again. But then I felt his hand pull me into his lap. He kissed me passionately and then we just sat there in each others arms, no words, for a long time.

He finally said "let's get out of here." I agreed and we left through the back door.

He took me to the Hyatt downtown where he had a room on the top floor overlooking the city and he ordered dinner and champagne. I loved it when he took control, assuming that I would love whatever decision he made for us. I always did. That night was no different. Everything that existed in my life just twenty four hours earlier no longer existed; there was Paul and only Paul. For the rest of that night, we had sex with all the verve we usually did. He was looking hot with his bronzed skin and his hair had turned redder from exposure to the sun. He told me that he had moved to Miami and he wanted me to join him. He was very excited about his new life and wanted me to be in it.

Chapter 15

Miami was an interesting place, exciting, warm and very different from home. Paul actually lived in Miami Beach on the south end, it was beautiful. The hotel he lived in sat directly on the beach and at night you could hear the waves crashing to shore. I spent most of the first weeks laying in the sun on the pool deck and walking around investigating all the sights this place had to offer. I soon became bored though, I had nothing to do and each day Paul would go to work and not return till sometimes twelve hours later and sometimes not until the next day. I didn't ask too many questions, he seemed really tense at times. Our sex wasn't as good as I had hoped, either. We were not engaging in the sex I craved, the sex I needed to feel alive. He wasn't as attentive and sexy with me as he had been back home. That was the Paul I needed; why had he changed; what had I done? When he was away, all I thought about was him and what I would do to please him and when I was with him all I could do was try to please him.

I was regularly smoking pot and had made a few acquaintances near the hotel that I smoked with. I occasionally hooked up with some Quaaludes and Paul always brought home some cocaine for us to use. My body had taken on a soft bronze color from the sun and my red hair had turned strawberry blonde. Boredom is a dangerous place for an addict. I was becoming more and more restless; I wanted to go home. I needed some stimulation. This was no life for me. I shared my feelings of restlessness with Paul and he just blew it off and told me to make some friends. He was becoming more distant and he would not give me the attention I craved. We had ceased going out and having fun. I became more needy and he came home less. My using increased and so did my loneliness.

One night, about four months after I had moved there, Paul came home in a rage about something. I was sitting on the bed snorting some lines and smoking a joint. He took the joint from me and took a hit which he inhaled deeply. He stood there for a moment and accused me of using all his stash, I was stunned, then he pulled me off the bed by my hair and pushed me to my knees he loosened his pants and mounted me from behind with a new level of violence that I had not experienced with him. This was not sexual; this was vicious. It felt vicious. I was not excited, I was afraid. When he finished he got up fastened his pants and pulled me to my feet and hit me hard across my face, I fell backwards onto the bed. He grabbed me again and started hitting me, I was able to get loose and I started to run to the door and he grabbed my arm and threw me against the wall which I hit with a loud thud. My mouth was bleeding and my head was confused by his sudden outburst of violence. He then pulled off his belt and started beating me. I fell to the floor and then started to crawl away from him. He caught me by the hair and pulled me back and continued to hit me with his belt. Each smack hurt more. What had I done, why was he doing this; I could not figure it out. A knock on the door startled Paul and he stopped long enough for me to make it to my feet and lock myself in the bathroom. I was more afraid than I had ever been.

I grabbed a towel to wipe my bloody mouth and sat down on the floor with my back to the door and started to sob. I could hear voices but could not hear what they were saying and then I heard the door close. It was quiet except for Paul's movement towards the bathroom door. I felt him lean against the door and then heard the sound of him sliding down towards the floor. I sensed him there just on the other side of this wooden door, the only sounds were the sounds of my sobs.

A long time passed and then I heard Paul get up and leave the room. I was still afraid and I sat there for a few minutes to make sure he was not coming right back. I got up and washed my face which had become swollen and painful. My body was marked with welts from head to toe. I carefully opened the bathroom door, went to the closet and slipped into a pair of jeans and a t-shirt. I grabbed my suitcase and threw my things into it, grabbed my purse and what little money was sitting on the dresser. I left my key and a note which simply read, "Goodbye Paul."

Chapter 16

That night I went to visit the only person in Miami who was a friend of sorts, the bartender at the hotel next door. I walked into the bar, suitcase in hand, swollen face – I looked a wreck. Mack looked up and saw me; his smile immediately changed to a look of concern. I put my suitcase down near the bar and sat on one of the stools. He came over immediately with a bottle of Jack and a shot glass. "What's up little one?" is all he said as he poured the first shot. I grabbed the shot, poured it down my throat and slammed the glass on the bar motioning to Mack to pour another, an activity I repeated four more times. My head was spinning from the five successive shots and the pain of my swollen face. It was late and the bar was quiet. Mack would be closing up soon, I didn't know what I was going to do next but I didn't really care, thanks to the Jack.

I must have blacked out because the next thing I knew I was at Mack's place naked in his bed. He was snoring and naked, too. I felt sick. I carefully slipped out of the bed and made it to the bathroom. I leaned over the toilet and puked my guts out. I didn't think I would ever stop. I hadn't been this sick in a long time. I climbed into the shower and just let the warm water run over me for a while trying to get straight. I was standing with my face against the wall my eyes closed and suddenly I felt Mack press his body against mine. He took the bar of soap and ran it over my back and my ass, pausing there and then running his fingers in the crack and up into my vagina. It felt good, I moaned. He then leaned down and kissed the back of my neck, running his tongue up into my ear, nibbling at the lobe. I leaned my body back into him inviting his penis to penetrate me. He entered me with gentle strokes lifting me up off the floor of the shower. My moans grew louder and louder till I was screaming with pleasure. The warm water was running over us and added to the excitement of the sex. Mack was moaning too and then he started slamming into me with a force that made him orgasm.

Mack let me stay for a couple of days till the bruises lightened on my face anyway then he gave me some cash and an address of a body painting studio that was run by someone he knew. I had reached a new low, but a girl has to eat. So I went to the body painting place and they hired me on the spot. The rules were simple, you let the guy paint your body but no sex, certainly not without the boss' approval and a lot more money, which most of these guys didn't have. The other women that worked there seemed nice but they had all been hardened from this life long ago. One of them, a young woman named Paige, invited me to stay with her and I gave her most of the cash I had to share this dump she lived in that was a few blocks from the studio.

I worked there for about two weeks and one day after work the boss showed up at our apartment and asked me not to return to the studio. He did not say why and I was devastated. If I couldn't even do this for a job what would I do? I later found out from one of the girls that Paul had asked the owner to fire me. I guess he thought I would come crawling back to him if I had no place to go. I was still hurt and very angry and there was no way I was going back. I had a few bucks and Paige said I could stay till the end of the month.

The next day I was walking along Collins Avenue and I met a man who claimed to be a photographer named Alex and he said he would like to do some photos of me. We talked for a while and I had become convinced he was fairly harmless; so I went with him to his studio.

The studio was located on the second floor above a liquor store right on Collins Avenue. It was a large room which was furnished with only a bed, a TV, and his photographic equipment, and the bathroom doubled as a dark room. I stretched out on the bed and Alex shot a couple of photos and then offered me some tequila to help me relax. We drank the tequila straight out of the bottle and smoked some very good hash; I got relaxed.

I was feeling light and free and the shoot was becoming fun. A female friend of his dropped by and got in on the shoot and we created some pretty provocative photos, I was having a good time. I was no longer distracted by my troubles. I knew I would never reap any rewards from the pictures taken that day, but being fairly screwed up I didn't really care.

Alex did do one really great thing for me the next day; he introduced me to Jon, who owned a night club in Ft. Lauderdale.

Jon liked me immediately and invited me to stay in Ft. Lauderdale with him. He had a lovely apartment above the club which was located just across the street from the beach. Jon was about forty five, had long silver hair. He was six feet tall and was very attractive. He had a very fit body and a very dirty mind. We had lots of sex and he kept me as happy as he could. I was his new toy, the object of his affection, and he loved to show me off to his friends, a true trophy.

Chapter 17

Each morning I would wake to the sun streaming in the bay window that looked out on to the beach; Jon always pulled up the blinds when he left. I was usually not as eager to get up as he was. I loved his bed and I loved his bedroom; it was very masculine yet very warm at the same time. His bed was an iron four-poster with a dark brown lambskin blanket. The room had honey-colored hardwood floors and Oriental carpets in colors of chocolate, sapphire, olive and wine. There was an olive green leather sofa, a corresponding love seat and an iron coffee table that matched the bed. A fully stocked wet bar was built into the wall by the large walk-in closet. Across the room was the bathroom, which was almost as big as the bedroom. In one corner was a large porcelain tub and in the opposite corner was a large shower built for two. In between the shower and the tub was a marble countertop with two porcelain sinks. A large beveled mirror hung on the wall above each sink. The ceiling contained a large skylight which brought wonderful sunlight into the room which was disturbing as often as it was pleasant.

Some mornings the trip to the bathroom was longer than others due to the hangover I had as the result of the activities the night before. I usually paused at the wet bar for a gulp of vodka before climbing into the shower. I would then put on my bikini top and some cutoffs and head down to the beach with a joint in hand. Jon was usually downstairs at the bar taking care of business; dealing with employees and vendors. I always stopped to say hello and give him a kiss and he always paused for me, but for only a few seconds.

Jon was a beautiful man and I loved to watch him. I loved the way he would just stand there, serious look on his face that would erupt into a smile suddenly when he saw me. His colorful silk shirts would fall softly against his well-built frame; his firm ass always looked wonderful in tight jeans. He had an air of confidence that made him irresistible and he loved tantalizing all of my senses; which he did without effort. I was intoxicated by him. I would do anything he asked.

Sex was different with him than with Paul or Michael, Jeff and Alberto. It was driven by the mind. Jon was the man who proved to me that ecstasy was eighty percent mental and only twenty percent physical. He told me: "It is the mental that drives the physical; it is the mental that makes the physical more enjoyable. It is the mental that makes absolute pleasure possible. It is so much more than the physical act alone can ever be."

Jon was assertive, not aggressive; he never hit me or engaged in any sado-masochist games with me, but he liked to command my actions and I would obey. It was a powerful and seductive game that I enjoyed playing and it was all I thought about most of my waking hours. It was intoxicating and I loved it. He liked it when I would describe in detail how much I wanted him and he would then describe in great detail how much he desired me. He loved to watch the orgasm well up inside me until I would shudder and scream. Then he would whisper in my ear and kiss my neck and watch my hips rise up off the bed inviting him, begging him.

I could never get enough of him.

Chapter 18

One day I borrowed Jon's Jaguar and went to Boca Raton to do some shopping. It was a pretty day, the skies were clear and the temperature was about eighty five degrees. I had the top down and the radio blasting. I had smoked a joint before I left and I was feeling good. I pulled into the downtown area and found a parking space along the main street.

The loud music caught the attention of two handsome men who were dining on the patio of the café next to where I had parked. They both smiled; and I waved. One of them motioned for me to join them and I decided that would be fun; after all, Jon would be busy and wouldn't miss me.

I had always enjoyed the attention of handsome men, it made me excited. I especially liked it when men would watch me, their eyes looking away as I would catch them, although some would choose to just continue to watch me even though they had been caught; this was especially exciting and it was no different on this occasion. I could feel their eyes as they watched me open the door and step out, walk around and deposit my coins into the parking meter, turn the handle and then walk towards them. I could feel their eyes on every flexed muscle of my tanned legs up to the hem of my short black slip dress. I could see their smiles of enjoyment as they observed my ankle strap high heels walking closer to them. I had my hair pulled back but the wind had caught a few curls and they were falling around my face. When I reached their table, I extended my hand and introduced myself as they both stood up. The first gentleman took my hand and put a soft kiss on it and said his name was Carlos then he introduced his friend Lupe. Lupe also took my hand and kissed it softly as he looked up at me with his big dark eyes. Carlos pulled out a chair for me to sit on and motioned to the waiter. I sat between them; we formed a semi circle around the café table that was in the back corner of the patio. By the time the waiter brought the third drink, Carlos had his hand on my thigh; and by the time the fifth drink arrived he had his fingers in my vagina. The pleasure was incredible, and I could not keep from spreading my legs over the sides of the chair, I wanted him to go deeper; I wanted more.

Since I had been with Jon I had not been so bold as to go with another man. I was quite drunk and I knew my inhibitions had evaporated. Then I blacked out. The next thing I was aware of was being with Carlos in his studio. I was lying naked on his bed and he was painting my picture. What time was it, what day was it? I didn't know how much time had passed or what had transpired between us; but we both seemed contented. What about Jon, the Jag, I wondered – but I had no answers and I knew he would be concerned about his car by now. Fear of the unknown consumed me and I had to move. Carlos was surprised by my sudden personality change. I tried to explain that I needed to get the car back and he told me he understood. "We will finish another time" is all he said as he handed me my dress and shoes.

Only a few hours had actually passed and I was still a little drunk but I managed to navigate my way back to Ft. Lauderdale without incident. Jon was waiting for me and observed that I had no packages, disappointment showed on his face but he didn't say a word. I told him I needed to shower, and I excused myself. I reappeared some forty minutes later dressed for dinner. We met up with some of his friends for dinner at a private club and Jon never asked me where I had been. That night we had sex in the most violent manner we had ever had; he entered me roughly and continued to give it to me roughly. Anger is a very powerful emotion; it kept Jon excited for a long time and by morning I did not want to get up from the bed. I was sore from head to toe.

Pain was obviously the price I paid for my indiscretion. I felt remorse for what I had done and I poured myself another drink.

Chapter 19

Jon started to tire of me, I had been drinking a lot and was looking a bit old and tired; one day he came to me and gave me some money to go home. He didn't really say that he wanted me to leave and not come back, but I knew that is what he wanted in his heart. I was no longer the object of his desires. I had become a pain in the ass, and an embarrassment. Even I could see that. I was saddened by his decision and yet relieved by his letting me go. So I collected my things and left. I was now twenty-five and had no job, no place to live and no real goals.

When I went back I went back to the home I grew up in. My parents had mixed emotions about seeing me. They loved me, but they were helpless when it came to my drinking and drugging. Neither of them really understood me; not that they ever really tried. I was entering into one of the darkest periods of my life and I didn't see it coming. Maybe my parents did, but they could not stop it. Even their love could not have prevented the pain I was about to experience.

I had never really grown up; I was just a little girl in a woman's body. I functioned in the adult world but my emotions were those of a child. The pain of Jon's rejection turned into anger which I turned inward to self loathing. I was devastated. I had spent years trying to leave and now I was back. Back to a place that had always made me feel small and insignificant. I had been living big in the past few years and returning to my small life in my parent's home just made me drink even more. I needed to anaesthetize myself. I needed oblivion.

I was dying and I didn't even know it.

Chapter 20

The money Jon had given me ran out in a short period of time and I started looking for work. I did not have much ambition at the time, I just needed something to keep me busy and finance my bad habits and the small studio apartment I had rented in the university district. I found a job in the office of a very nice furniture store owned by a man named Peter Cox, Cox and Son Furniture.

Peter was a very handsome older gentleman, married with a son named David who was about twenty four years old. David showed up at the store pretty much when he wanted to, so Peter never really counted on him. There were a couple of salesmen on the staff and a bookkeeper who worked only two days a week. I worked five days a week from noon to eight, which really helped with the hangovers I was having on a daily basis. I was still healthy enough to pull myself together by noon and make it through the day. When I got off at eight I would go to my favorite bar and party till closing.

I worked with Peter for about a month before he started flirting with me. I would flirt with him as well. One night we were alone in the store, Peter was feeling a bit down and I was in one of my party moods. I was dancing around the store showing off, trying to get him to cheer up. I was on the opposite side of the store when I turned the music up slightly; Patsy Cline's "Crazy" filled the store with a melancholy sound. I swayed to the soft beat rubbing my hands over my breasts, head tilted back, eyes closed, enjoying the music in the moment.

Peter was sitting at his desk watching me and it was exciting to watch him watch me. I got closer to him and started moving my hips – teasing him, inviting him. He reached out to and pulled me into his lap and started kissing me. It felt good; he was so gentle. I was still moving to the music that was playing, softly brushing my breasts against him.

Suddenly someone opened the front door and stepped into the store. Peter jumped up, knocking me to the floor. I sat there startled for a moment then pulled myself up off the floor and sat down at his desk. It was a customer who needed to drop off some fabric swatches that she had borrowed a week earlier. Peter greeted her with his usual warm friendly smile asking her if she had made a decision. They shared ideas for a few minutes and then she left. It was almost eight so Peter locked the front door and dimmed the showroom lights before returning to his desk.

The original mood had been lost but Peter took my hand a pulled me up from the chair into his arms and kissed me on the lips. I moved into the kiss; it was exciting and I liked it. He ran his hand down my back and slowly drew my dress up, exposing my ass. I was really excited now and I could feel the wetness between my legs. He lifted me up onto the counter, pulling my legs around his waist. He unfastened his trousers and dropped them to the floor. I wiggled out of my panties and invited him to penetrate me. It felt good. It did not take him long to orgasm and it was so powerful for him he fell back into his chair when he was done. I remained on the counter feeling a bit cheated by the short experience.

After a few minutes I jumped off the counter, stepped back into my panties, grabbed my purse and left Peter sitting there in his chair with a stunned looked on his face. The only thing I had in my mind now was getting to oblivion as fast as I could and I headed for my usual bar, Blue, in search of new companions, which I always managed to find. Tonight was no different.

The bar was packed, unusual for this early hour but there were a lot of new faces in there. It looked as though there were at least a dozen young men who were celebrating some kind of event. I squeezed through them to the bar and asked Charlene to pour me my usual. Jack Daniels straight up with an ice water back. Charlene flipped a double shot glass off the shelf and set it on the bar, grabbed the bottle of Jack from the premium rack and poured me a double; by the time she got the ice water to the bar, I had gulped the first drink and was asking for another. She poured one more double for me before I wandered away with my ice water.

I could hear some of the young guys giving Charlene a hard time as I strolled towards the pool tables. The Jack had gone to my head and I was feeling invincible. There were a couple of young guys playing pool and I asked if I could join in for a game, they looked up and smiled. I grabbed a cue stick from the wall and almost tripped getting back to the table. They laughed and asked me to break. I hit the cue ball with a firm steady bang and spread the balls all over the table. Not one went into the pocket though. "Okay boys, go for it!" I said as I leaned against the table for stability. The first young man, Jason, took a shot but instead of concentrating on the table he was looking at me and missed getting a ball in a pocket. Then Todd bellied up to the table, cue stick in hand and leaned over the table next to me rubbing his thigh on mine. He managed to knock a solid ball in the corner pocket and then moved to the other side of the table. He missed the second shot and it was my turn again. Todd gave me a wink and said "it's all yours honey, good luck. What are you drinking anyway?" He walked to the bar and got a beer and a shot of Jack for me.

I was feeling pretty full of myself and I raised the cue stick and hit a stripe into the side pocket, then another into the corner, then another, and another;

Todd and Jason just stood there, mouths open. "Wow! That's pretty good little lady" Jason said as he lit a cigarette. Then I missed the last shot and had to give up my turn. So close but not good enough. I swallowed the shot and tossed the glass to Todd. He went to the bar and got another for me. When he brought it back, he came up behind me pressing himself against my ass and reached around me to hand me the shot. His tight body felt good and I leaned back into him.

The Jack had definitely gone to my head and I knew I was about to be transported to that magical place where space and time become seamless.

I don't know how much longer we played pool but the next thing I was aware of was Todd's tongue down my throat. I was in his arms and we were kissing like a couple of teenagers. I could feel Todd's excitement and mine. I pulled away briefly to get a glimpse of where we were, I knew we weren't in the bar playing pool any longer. I could sense that the place we were in was a lot less public and a lot more isolated. Todd was tugging at my dress trying to pull it off me at the same time he was trying to step out of his boots. We were both a bit drunk and wobbly and Todd lost his balance and we both tumbled to the floor. Todd pushed himself up onto his knees and then unfastened his pants; pulling them off to expose an amazing hard on. He had a beautiful body and a penis to match. He jammed his penis in my mouth and after a few moments I went back into a blackout.

The next thing I was aware of was laying there on the floor feeling pretty used up and cold. I must have passed out. I sat up shivering; wondering where Todd was, where I was, what was this place? It was still dark out and the only light was the glow streaming in the open blinds from lights outside the building. I pulled myself off the floor by grasping a nearby chair and crawled towards the window. I got to my feet and looked outside to see if I recognized anything. There was a big neon sign that read "BIG ED'S USED CARS". I turned away from the window and looked around the room I was in; sure enough, it was the office of Big Ed's. "Great, this is fucking great!"

I stumbled around till I found a desk lamp, which I switched on and looked around for my purse, my coat, and the address of Big Ed's. I did not find my purse or coat, probably still at the bar. I was all the way across town from where I started the evening, and it was two in the morning anyway. I sat down in the desk chair and put my legs on the desk. I was somewhat sober but I did not know what to do. If I went outside I would freeze, I had no money for a cab. Peter was out of the question; but David wasn't.

I called David; he was home and still awake. I told him about my dilemma and he told me he would come get me if I would spend the rest of the night with him. He must have been shot down earlier by the woman he was putting the moves on. I definitely had to get out of this situation, so I agreed.

Chapter 21

David was his usual flirtatious self but with more of an edge. When I got into his car he offered me a hit of his hash pipe, it smelled good and tasted great. I felt a sense of relief as I released the smoke and watched it rise into the air towards the windshield.

I looked a mess, but David didn't seem to notice. He drove towards his apartment chatting away about the happenings of his night. I soon realized he was buzzing on cocaine and he was trying to smooth out the high with the hash. All I could think about was how much I needed a shot of something. The hash was good but a shot of Jack would be even better. I knew we would soon be at David's apartment and I could get what I needed. David was going on and on and the radio was blasting and I wanted to crawl out of my skin. I felt shame over the earlier happenings of the evening since I did not know what had really happened and now I was with David, who was anywhere except with me. It was all so strange.

We pulled into the parking lot of his apartment building and he parked in the space close to the entrance. He jumped out and ran around the car to get the door for me. I turned towards the open door to step out and he took my hand to help me. I was surprised he was such a gentleman. After I was completely out of the car David reached into the glove box to retrieve a small package and then closed the door with a quick motion as he turned towards me and grabbed my hand pulling me towards the entrance of the building.

Once we were inside he put the package on the coffee table and headed for the kitchen. "What do you want to drink?" he asked as I heard him opening and closing drawers and cabinets. "Bring me some Jack straight up; better yet bring me the bottle," I said softly as I walked towards the kitchen. "What?" he yelled before he realized I was standing in the doorway watching him. "I said I will have a shot of Jack please." He grabbed a rocks glass from the dishwasher and poured me a double. I took a sip and immediately felt the chill leave my body as it was replaced by the warmth of the booze.

I wandered into the bathroom and finished the drink as I took off my dress and shoes and stepped into the shower. The warm water felt good on my cold achy body. I tilted my head back and let the shampoo run off my hair, down my back and over my ass. The combination of hash and whiskey made everything seem so surreal. I reached for the soap and lathered my body, rubbing my breasts and then running the soap down over my stomach and between my legs. I then put the bar of soap between my ass cheeks massaging the area gently and running my slippery hands over my ass as I let the bar of soap fall to the floor of the shower. I had my eyes closed enjoying my high when I heard the shower door open. David's naked body rubbed up against mine. He felt good. He managed to retrieve the soap and ran it over my back and then reached around me to rub my breasts. He then moved his hands slowly and deliberately down over my stomach and down between my thighs. I let out a soft moan inviting him to continue. He massaged my clitoris and was able to bring me to orgasm is a very short time.

David turned the water off and opened the shower door and pushed me to my knees on the bathroom floor and penetrated me from behind, his violent thrusts felt painfully luscious and he had me screaming in no time. I rolled over and he got on top of me. We went at it for what seemed like hours – on the floor, on the counter, on the sofa, in the bed – until we both passed out.

67

The daylight streaming in the window woke me up. I laid there for a moment wondering where I was and who I was with, my head was still foggy from the booze and drugs and I was having a hard time focusing on the surroundings that did not seem at all familiar. I rolled over onto my stomach and raised myself up on my elbows in time to see David's naked body holding two cups of coffee. Then the last ten hours of time flashed back through my mind. What was I doing? Why did I go on this way, day in and day out? It all seemed to be getting worse – the drinking, the drugs, the sex. How many more men will I invite into me today, tomorrow, the next day? What was going on with me and how come I could not stop?

David sat on the bed next to me and rubbed my ass and all the thoughts in my head evaporated like the steam coming off the coffee. I loved the feeling of being desired. I loved that he wanted to touch me, caress me, have sex with me; it was as intoxicating as the Jack I had been drinking the night before. I mood-altered with these feelings just the same way I mood-altered with booze and drugs. I could no longer just stay in my own being, I needed out, whatever it took – booze, drugs or sex!

I no longer knew what day it was or if I had to be somewhere other than where I was right then, and I did not care. I just wanted David to have sex with me again. I wanted to roll over on my back and welcome him into me. I did. He did. We stayed together all day and into the night, I can't remember how many times we had sex; it seemed like a lot. I was exhausted but we could not stop until the cocaine and Jack ran out.

I looked like hell and felt that way, too. David was a bit rough around the edges also; he had that deer in the headlights look on his face as he drove me over to Blue to pick up my car. He was kind enough to go in and get the keys from Charlene; I knew I was not capable of doing it.

Charlene had managed to hang on to my purse for the last couple of days but she did not know David, so she poked her head out the front door and I waved to her from the car. She had an awkward smile on her face as she handed my purse to David. He thanked her, ran back and tossed the purse into my lap as he got back into the car. I got out of David's car and fumbled with my purse trying to locate the car keys. I finally managed the door lock and dropped my tired body into the driver's seat. I adjusted the rearview mirror so I could see my face and I was shocked to see the woman looking back at me. I looked old and tired; I looked twice my age. My red hair had lost its shine, my face was pale and my eyes were dull. I could not even smile at myself any longer, all I felt was disgust.

It took me about five minutes to get the car started and in gear. David was long gone by then. I slowly drove out of the parking lot and headed for home.

Chapter 22

In the weeks that followed the night with David I don't know what was more painful, the constant attention I got from Peter or the lack of attention I got from David. I don't even know why I cared whether or not David paid attention to me; but I did. I had always been like that, no matter how many people liked me; I was always busy trying to win the attention and admiration of that one person who didn't. It was such a mystery.

I knew I needed rest and a good diet but instead I continued going to Blue every night; consuming my usual source of nutrition, alcohol.

Several times a week; Peter would pull me into his arms. I would feel his hard penis against my abdomen as he would pull my hair back and kiss my neck and breasts. We would usually end up having sex on his desk. He always seemed satisfied and I always left the store searching for oblivion, which I always found at Blue.

Some nights I could see the sadness in Charlene's face when she would see me stagger up to the bar and order shot after shot; but most nights I didn't care. I was losing all sense of self and all I wanted was to leave the planet. I could no longer live in my own skin. I wanted to feel differently than I was feeling. I was always searching for that state of nirvana, heaven, but the only thing I ever found was hell. I would drink until I was magically transported to some other place in space and time, which usually meant I would be naked somewhere with a man I did not know. And I didn't know how to stop.

I was aware of the pain of my existence but the only thing I could do for it was treat it with more alcohol, more drugs, more sex until I could no longer feel. That is what it was about all along – not feeling. It hurt too much to feel. To feel the pain of Paul, Michael, Jon, David. To feel the pain of losing all those little pieces of my soul, my heart, my flesh.

That hole in my soul was so big and so dark and the wind was blowing through it with an eerie howling sound. A sound that I needed to drown out.

Chapter 23

The deep knowledge of my soul sickness and the ache so big it consumed me, was more than I could bear. I no longer could escape through oblivion; there was only one choice left. This was one of the darkest days of my life and I knew what I needed to do, really leave this planet and the agony of my painful existence.

I was sick and shaking; it had been a while since my last drink and my mind was confused. I walked out into the cool night air – no coat, no shoes; I no longer cared about anything. My hair was tangled and my face was pale, my eyes echoed the emptiness of my soul. I was without hope.

I had not made it very far when I realized I could not go even one more step and I sat on the curb to rest. I was so tired. That was the last thing I remembered until I woke up the next morning in a soft comfortable bed in a strange blue room. Was I dreaming? Was I dead? Suddenly a noise from another room, the door opened and there stood my angel.

John was an angel. He found me lying on the sidewalk. Not knowing who I was or where I belonged he brought me to his home and put me to bed. He had brought me some hot tea and a croissant and asked me how I was feeling. I really felt like shit but I lied and told him I was fine. He was a gentle man and I could tell he was very kind. He was probably in his forties, with soft brown hair, green eyes that sparkled with life, and a crooked smile. His soft voice was very comforting as he explained to me how I had come to be in his home and in his guest bedroom.

I had trouble lifting the cup to my mouth as I was shaking almost violently; he reached over and helped me. The tea tasted good and the warmth filled my chest. I knew I was in a safe place. He laid a terry robe at the foot of the bed and left the room. I continued to lay there for a few minutes looking about the room. The furnishings were old and worn but very comforting.

As I got up from the bed still shaking and unsure of my footing; I could hear the opera music floating in the air. I was not a fan of opera but like everything else I had seen so far, it just added to my newfound comfort. I had trouble putting on the robe as I was so shaky and sick. I had to find a bathroom. I walked to the closed door and opened it, stuck my head out and looked both ways as if I was about to step into traffic. I saw several other doors, not knowing which one was the bathroom. I walked out into the hall and stared at each door, suddenly John's soft voice said "it's the door on the left." I jumped, said "thanks," as I walked to the door, went inside, and closed the door behind me. I immediately fell to my knees in front of the toilet and gagged. There was nothing in my stomach but I could not stop the heaves from rising up into my throat. I just knelt there until they stopped.

Sweating and shaking, I stepped into the large tub and ran cool water till it covered me. I so much wanted to just sink under the water and open my mouth, let it be the end; I was so tired. As my mind drifted into morbidity, John knocked on the door and asked if I needed anything. When I did not answer, he opened the door and stepped into the room. He had a look of concern on his face. I knew at that moment that John was an angel and he was there to help. He supervised my bath, helped me wash my hair, brought me a towel and aided my exit from the tub. I caught a glimpse of myself in the mirror and I hardly recognized the woman I had become. My thin bony body was pale like my face, my hair had lost its luster and my eyes were empty.

I put my robe back on and we went to the kitchen. It was a wonderful kitchen, filled with light and so much love. I could tell John loved to cook; this love was in every square inch of this sunny yellow kitchen. He pulled one of the Prague chairs away from the antique oak table and I sat down. John went to the refrigerator and brought out a pitcher of freshly squeezed orange juice and poured me a glass. I carefully lifted the glass to my mouth and took a small sip. My stomach was still queasy and I did not want to get the heaves again. I kept it down. John was busy taking a baking pan of hot scones from the oven and the air was filled with the fragrance of vanilla and cinnamon. "Smells wonderful" I choked out, as I tried to smile and appear normal. John smiled too, but it was genuine and warm. I felt welcomed in this unfamiliar home. John placed a lovely china plate in front of me and gently put one of the scones on it. I closed my eyes and remembered my grandmother's kitchen from long ago. I was shaking so much that I had trouble using the fork so I just broke off the corner and put the small piece in my mouth. I think it had been some time since I had eaten. "Take small bites" cautioned John, "you'll be all right". He sat across from me with his large coffee mug in silence for then next few minutes.

I could not understand why I felt so comforted by him or why I was not fearful here in this foreign house with this strange man. It was not like the times that I would come to in mysterious places with unknown people; it was like home. I felt secure, safe, cared for, like I had felt with Abe and Sheila. Who was he and why was he being so kind to me? He obviously did not know who I really was. The woman everyone was tiring of. The woman who only brought pain to those whose lives she touched. The woman whose soul had a hole so big that the wind blew fiercely through it like winds that blow in a deep canyon.

John broke the silence with a short summary of himself. He was a professor at the university and he and his long time partner Ken lived in this house, which had at one time belonged to his mother Aggie.

It was evident that many remnants of Aggie's presence remained there in the house giving it an eclectic flair.

Aggie had also been a professor at the university but had passed away some five years ago. The house was ideally located and he had always considered it home so he and Ken decided to move into it. Ken was an artist, whose beautiful watercolors decorated many of the walls. John's face lit up when he talked about Ken. He chatted about him as he led me through each room showing me his work; each piece had a story.

Ken was in Santa Fe, New Mexico, doing a gallery show of his latest works, which embodied the beautiful colors of the Southwest. John had photographs of each piece that had gone to the show. "I know he will sell them all" John said with an angelic smile on his face. The final painting he showed me was a nude of himself that Ken had done thirteen years earlier. He looked at it proudly as he pointed out how young he was then. It made me giggle with embarrassment. I had never seen anything like it before.

After the tour I felt good enough to get dressed and go home. John was reluctant and protested, he did not agree that I was well enough to make it even the few blocks to my home. I assured him that I was feeling great thanks to his help and he then insisted on walking me home.

Chapter 24

John had been my angel that day and continued to be my angel. He would stop by a couple of times each week and bring me soup, casseroles, scones, and vegetables. He would look at my gaunt face and then feed me some more. He would sit and watch me while I slowly swallowed each bite of his delicious food. I am positive that it was John who kept me alive during this time of my life. The drinking had definitely taken its toll on my body and my beauty had faded away. John's food was the only nutrition that I ingested and I was weak most of the time. My drinking made it impossible for me to show up for work so Peter fired me.

It was Tuesday, 7:00 PM and I am sitting on the bar stool at Blue tossing down my usual three shots with an ice water back. Charlene came in to do her shift and saw me holding myself up on the edge of the bar leaning on my bent arm which was keeping my head up. I had stopped the shakes, but the nausea was lingering and I did not think I would make it to the ladies' room. I was a mess and Charlene knew it. She came around the bar and helped me off the stool and took me to the ladies' room. I leaned over the sink and started to vomit. There was nothing inside of me except the whiskey I had just drunk. I choked and spit and blood started coming from my mouth, my hand slipped from the sink top and I fell backwards on to the floor hitting my head on the stall door on the way down. The last thing I saw and heard before I lost consciousness was Charlene's scared look and her frightened gasp.

The next thing I remember was waking up in a pale green room. I felt panicky as I looked around and saw the beeping machines and tubes attached to my arms. I knew I was in the hospital, but what happened, and why I was there were mysteries to me. My heart started to race as my anxiety grew and one of the machines started to beep loudly and a nurse burst through the door and rushed to my bedside. She told me to stay calm and then checked all my attachments, as she reached around me I caught a glimpse of her name tag, Sara. Sara was a middle aged brunette who spoke to me in a very soft voice "how are you feeling dear?" I wasn't sure how I felt exactly but I didn't feel good. My head hurt and I felt very nauseous. When I tried to sit up the movement of my head made me dizzy and I fell back against the pillows.

How long had I been here, hours, days, I did not know. It must have been nighttime as it was dark outside the window. "Where am I, how long have I been here?" I asked in a small frightened voice. "You are at Mercy Hospital and you were brought here on Tuesday" was Sara's response. She said Tuesday, that must mean it is another day, other than Tuesday! "What day is it now Sara?" I asked as my anxiety grew stronger, the machine beeping loudly once again. "Stay calm, I'll tell you everything" Sara whispered. Sara leaned over me and checked my vitals carefully, looking into my eyes. "It is Saturday and your two friends have been here every day." My two friends, I have two friends; went through my mind as I blurted out, "who?" "Your friend John and your friend Charlene who came here with you in the ambulance" Sara said, "They have been waiting for you to wake up, I'll get them as soon as I finish here."

John and Charlene, my friends, they have been waiting for me to wake up for days, I could not believe it. How is it that people can care that much for me when I cannot care that much for myself. I was amazed.

As Sara continued checking me over she told me that I had gone into a coma due to the head injury I sustained from the fall which was the result of my weakness, intense dehydration, and a bleeding esophagus which was a result of my drinking. She said it all with kindness and grace.

Sara left the room quietly and a few minutes later John and Charlene came through the door. Charlene smiled sweetly as if she were seeing a loved one. John just stood there staring at me with a look of relief on his face. They were both quiet for a long moment and then John broke the silence with "are you hungry?" Charlene and I looked at him and started to laugh. "John, you're such a mama" is all I could say.

How blessed I was to have both of them in my life.

I had to stay in the hospital for another few days. The head injury did not seem very serious but the doctors wanted to observe me, and the bleeding esophagus seemed to be healing just fine. Of course the doctors told me to stop drinking, which I conceded to be good advice.

On the following Wednesday, they released me from the hospital and John came to pick me up. He had packed my things and moved them along with me to his guest room. I know John did this because he loved me but I felt ashamed. I felt like a little girl who could not take care of herself.

Ken was on an east coast tour which would take him to Boston, New York, Atlanta, and finally Miami. He had shows in each city and John was starting to miss him a lot. He decided to join Ken in Miami and invited me along. I was sure he just wanted to keep an eye on me. I had been living with him for about six weeks now and had managed to stay sober. This was the longest stretch of sober time I had had in years. I was looking good, color had returned to my face and my red curls had shine to them again, my green eyes looked alive. Not only had John been feeding me well but he made me go for long walks each day. I felt vibrant and strong. I was ready for a trip to the beach.

Chapter 25

We arrived in Miami International Airport on Tuesday, 11:25 AM. It was a beautiful day, the temperature was about eighty five degrees and there was a slight breeze blowing from the northeast. The air smelled sweet with the fragrance of orange blossoms. Ken was waiting at the gate when we got off the plane and greeted John with a warm loving embrace. He gave me a peck on the cheek and reached for the small suitcase I had in my hand, "let me carry that for you". I smiled and released my grip on the handle. John was so excited, he chatted endlessly all the way to the baggage claim area, not letting Ken get a word in. Ken just listened with a look of love on his face. Yes, these two were so right for each other, definitely in love, definitely friends.

Ken drove us along Collins Avenue towards North Miami Beach where he was staying. The woman who owned the gallery, Loretta Bernard, had a beautiful guest house on her estate and was thrilled to have a guest like Ken, who was smart, funny, and talented. She also let him use her 1957 Thunderbird convertible, baby blue of course. My red curls were blowing in the air as we drove along the beach and I was able to catch a glimpse of the waves crashing to shore between the tall buildings that stretched out like beads of a necklace.

The beach made me think of Paul. My mind wandered to the days that were good with us. I got lost in my thoughts and I had to reach between my legs to calm the excitement that accompanied my memories. Then I remembered the beating and tears rolled down my cheeks. I brushed them away and returned to the present to hear John calling to me from the front seat, "do you want to get something to eat?" "You're awfully quiet back there." "Just enjoying the drive" is all I could manage to get out. Ken suggested the restaurant at one of the hotels on the beach and we decided to stop.

As I got out of the car I could smell the wonderfully familiar scent of the ocean. I loved that smell. Today it made me feel happy and sad. Happy to be here with the one man I was truly loved by, John; and sad for not enjoying the happiness that John and Ken had together. Would I ever experience that kind of love and joy? Was it just an illusion for a woman like me. Just then I felt the warm loving embrace of John, "Are you okay kiddo?" "Yes, very okay!" I blurted out. "Good, very good" he said as he pulled me close to him and held me for a few minutes while enjoying the warm breeze that came up from the shore.

Ken had gone inside to see if we could get a table on the patio. I was glad that Ken wanted to sit on the patio because I did not want to go inside and leave the warmth of the sun and the fresh smell of the beach. I was also enjoying the sounds of the surf and the seagulls calling to each other as they flew overhead. The patio area had round tables with umbrellas and sat a level above the pool deck. We watched the hotel guests lying in the sun on comfy patio lounges with fluffy white towels.

The scent of suntan lotion brought back memories of my days in Miami and Ft. Lauderdale. I once again drifted into the euphoria of those days, forgetting the bad times. I missed that carefree time of my life and the fun I had had, but most of all I missed the sex. Paul, Jon, Max, Carlos, sex, sex and more sex.

My eyes were closed and my mind was racing, I actually let out a soft moan before I realized that I had drifted away from the conversation and company of John and Ken. I had been a good girl for long enough I thought, I need some fun too! My heart ached to be with someone, someone who would transport me to the wonderful place of total oblivion, mesmerizing sex!

John and Ken were chatting of galleries and shops, restaurants and hotels. I wanted to be a part of their conversation but could not release my fantasies. They had absorbed my attention and I was feeling quite horny and restless.

Although I could hear the voices of John and Ken, their conversation did not bring me back to the table from my thoughts but the arrival of the waiter did. He put the menu down in front of me and gently placed the linen napkin on my lap, I was startled and when I looked up I saw the face of Rick. A beautiful face it was, golden tan, blonde hair, brown eyes, and a smile that made me freeze in the moment. 'Welcome to Miami, what can I get you to drink?" I was about to say "Jack Daniels" when John shot me a look of concern. "Ice tea, please" came out of my mouth instead. John smiled with a sense of relief. It had been eleven and a half weeks since I last had a shot of Jack. I missed it. It had been longer than that since I had sex and I was more than on the edge. I could actually understand that I could not drink because it was killing me but having sex was different. I really needed some sex. I needed to escape from my sadness, my loneliness, my feelings of not being enough; good enough, pretty enough, sexy enough! I knew everything would be different if I just had some sex. I would no longer ache when I watched others so happy; kissing, embracing each other with joy. I knew it would be different this time, I would find my Prince, I would find the one who would love and protect me.

Our waiter, Rick, returned to the table with our drinks and as he placed my ice tea down in front of me he shot me a big smile and a wink. I blushed as I smiled back. It felt as though he knew what I had been thinking about. He looked so handsome standing there in his tight black trousers and blue polo shirt with the hotel logo on the chest. He had a white linen apron around his waist which he pulled his order pad from as he asked if we were ready to order. I could not take my eyes off of him, he was so beautiful. I was suddenly so warm. I could not tell if it was the sight of Rick or the early afternoon sunshine. I slipped off the jacket I had on over my sundress, exposing my white skin. "The sun here in Miami Beach will scorch your lovely skin, make sure to protect yourself" Rick said. I blushed again, feeling vulnerable as I nodded.

Ken interrupted the moment by asking about one of the appetizers on the menu and Rick directed his attention to Ken. I was happy for the moment to collect myself so I could order. I had not felt so flustered by a man in a very long time, probably not since I took my first drink, anyway. I could feel my hands trembling as I looked down at the menu trying to remember what it was that I wanted to order. I was no longer hungry. I had butterflies in my stomach. Suddenly John, Ken, and Rick were all looking at me, "what?" I squeaked out. "Did you decide?" Rick asked, ready to write down my order. "What do you suggest?" my voice cracking, Rick replied that the Pompano was his favorite. "Pompano it is" I said with a big smile. John and Ken both ordered and as Rick headed for the kitchen I excused myself and headed for the ladies' room. Once inside the restaurant I scanned around the room for the restroom sign. Rick came up behind me and pointed towards the lobby of the hotel as he whispered in my ear "down the hall on the right." My knees went weak as I paused for a brief moment before walking towards the lobby. Once inside the ladies' room, I walked over to the sink and splashed my face with cold water.

Chapter 26

Ken's show opened on Wednesday at 7:00 pm. The Bernard Gallery was in downtown Miami just off Flagler in the art district. I was looking forward to going because I had not seen Ken's newest work yet. I could tell John was quite excited also, he always chatted on and on when he was excited.

I had relaxed in the sunshine by Loretta's swimming pool early in the day and my skin had taken on a little color. After a wonderful lunch of fresh stone crabs and a salad of baby greens, orange slices, honey roasted walnuts and blue cheese, on the patio with Loretta, Ken, and John; I went shopping with Loretta in the baby blue Thunderbird. I loved driving along the beach with the wind whipping through my curls making them dance.

Loretta had her hair pulled back under a colorful blue and yellow silk scarf which looked beautiful against her dark skin. She had big brown eyes and soft full red lips. She had on royal blue silk slacks with a matching silk blouse which hung softly on her small shapely frame. Her yellow beaded bracelet and earrings matched her yellow sandals.

Being with Loretta reminded me of Sheila. I drifted into memories of the wonderful times shared with Sheila and how much I loved and missed her. Then I drifted into thoughts of Abe, Paul – tears rolled down my cheeks. I brushed them away, leaned forward and turned up the radio. Loretta was listening to a Latin station and the music made me move my shoulders and snap my fingers. Loretta looked over at me and we both let out a laugh. "Do you like to dance?" asked Loretta. "I do, yes, I love to dance." I smiled and felt a flutter of excitement, it had been a while since I danced and had a fun at a club. "I'll take you to a wonderful club tonight after Ken's show – we'll do some real dancing!" Loretta said as she let out another laugh.

Loretta found a parking spot along the curb just outside of Burdines in Coconut Grove; she had little trouble sliding the baby blue Thunderbird into it. She pulled the scarf from her head pushed it into her purse and said "Let's go shopping!" Shopping we did, Loretta bought several dresses and shoes to match, I bought a dress and a pair of shoes for the show. It was simple but very elegant and flattering to my thin body. We had a café con leche at a local Cuban sandwich shop and drove back to Miami Beach.

Chapter 27

Ken and John were both very excited about the opening of the show and were dressed and waiting for us by 5:30 PM. Loretta was at the pool bar pouring white wine. As I reached for a glass, I thought to myself that it would be different this time; this time I would control it. I took a small sip and wandered off with my glass of wine towards the guest house to shower and dress for the evening. I had taken a few more sips before getting in the shower and as the warm water ran over my head and down my body I could feel how lightheaded I had become. It felt good. I also became painfully aware of how much I needed to have sex; I missed it so much and I longed to be held, touched, and penetrated. As I rubbed the bath sponge over my body I closed my eyes and imagined hands, strong hands, beautiful hands, sliding over my breasts, caressing my ass, penetrating my vagina, I could feel the waves of excitement fill me. It felt good. I felt good. I rubbed my clitoris with both hands until I came with a thunder that took me to my knees. I felt relieved and frustrated at the same time.

As I stepped from the shower, I saw my reflection in the full length mirror. I looked good, my body had taken on a bronze glow from the sun and although I was still quite thin, my shape had returned. My face looked young and well rested. I wrapped the towel around my wet head and stepped over to the sink to brush my teeth.

I was glad that I did not have to compete with John or Ken for the bathroom and I could take my time making myself beautiful. I applied lotion, cream, perfume, blush, mascara, and hot red lipstick. I shook my hair and decided to let it dry in the evening sun on the pool deck. I put on my robe and took my half glass of white wine and stepped out on to the porch. John and Ken were sitting in the shaded area under the ceiling fan near the main house on the opposite end of the pool. John waved and smiled; I waved back. I sat on the step of the porch and let the sun caress me. It did not take long for my hair to dry. I finished my glass of wine and stepped back into the guest cottage to dress.

My new dress looked beautiful as its light fabric fell softly over my body. It had a wide, low neckline and small cap sleeves and its acid green color looked shockingly wonderful against my skin and red hair. I stepped into my new matching shoes, grabbed my clutch bag and walked out onto the pool deck. Both John and Ken stood up as they saw me walking towards them, "You look smashing my dear" John said as he smiled his biggest, broadest smile. "I agree. Turn around let me look at you. Stunning, absolutely stunning; don't you just love Miami!" Ken said with a joyful tone. We all looked at each other and let out wonderful belly laughs. Just then Loretta appeared in the doorway and said "Let's party!"

Chapter 28

Loretta had her chauffer pick us up in the Mercedes limousine and we went off to the show in style. When we arrived in front of the gallery, the Miami Herald photographer was poised and ready to snap pictures of Ken and Loretta.

Loretta stepped from the limousine just like a movie star, dark glasses, Coco Channel dress in hot pink, matching shoes, clutch, and scarf in her left hand. The chauffer took her right hand and helped her from the car, the camera flashed several times as Loretta smiled broadly greeting everyone in her path warmly and sincerely. She is an amazing woman; so many people love her, Ken was so lucky to have had her approval of his work. Next Ken climbed out of the limousine. He looked like an excited little boy, a bit shy – yet overjoyed! The photographer snapped several shots of Ken's exit and then asked him to pose with Loretta in front of the gallery. Both of them had wonderful smiles and they looked fabulous! I sat in the limousine and watched, I felt so happy for both of them and John too, who was sitting there taking it all in as well.

John and I decided to get out of the Mercedes while everyone was distracted by Loretta and Ken. We stepped off to the side waiting for the pictures to be taken. Ken and Loretta finally entered the gallery along with the guests who had been waiting for them outside, John and I slipped in with the crowd. Joseph, Loretta's assistant, had done a wonderful job with the party. There was a long table in the colors of the Painted Desert with beautiful foods from the Southwest; wait staff carrying trays of champagne, a small ensemble playing soft Latin music, and of course all Ken's work adorning every wall in the room. The lighting made each piece take on an ethereal appearance. "Wow!" I said to John in a soft voice, he looked at me and said "I know, wow!" We both walked around wanting to giggle with glee for Ken, this was all so amazing. He had definitely arrived in the art world.

Photographers and reporters from several art publications arrived and Ken and Loretta were busy posing for them. People started to arrive, lots of people, beautiful people, important people, wealthy people, other artists, all to see Ken's amazing works of art. How wonderful for him! Tears welled up inside me I was so happy for this beautiful man and for my dear sweet friend John who loved him so much.

I reached for a glass of champagne and decided to step back and watch the guests observe Ken's work and listen to them chat about art and books and such, which reminded me of the times I spent at gallery parties with Sheila. The thought of Sheila's red lips smiling and chatting made me smile. I then thought about Abe which always brought me to the thought of Paul. That asshole, how I adored him and hated him at the same time.

Just as my thoughts were about to take a sad turn, I felt a tap on my shoulder. The tap shocked me out of my thoughts. I turned quickly to discover Rick the waiter standing there with a big smile on his face. "I was hoping to see you again" he said. "What?" was the only word I could manage and then he leaned down and kissed me on the neck and whispered "you are the most beautiful, exciting woman in this room." My knees went weak, that warm feeling exploded between my legs, my eyes closed, at that moment I wanted him to take me in his strong arms and penetrate me the way Paul did. I was completely shaken by the kiss; my hunger for sex was so strong. Maybe it was just the champagne, the excitement of the evening. I fell against him and he caught me with a gentle grip on my arm. "I'm sorry, it must be the champagne and my empty stomach" I apologized. "Don't worry, let's get something to eat." Rick took my arm and led me to the buffet table. So many luscious foods to choose from! I filled a small plate and walked over to the stairs that led up to Loretta's office. I sat on the second step and picked at the lovely treats. Rick joined me and we both sat there in silence for a few moments enjoying the food. He broke the silence by asking me if I were related to the artist. "No, Ken and John are good friends of mine; we are all staying in Loretta's guest house at the moment. Isn't she fantastic?" I said. Rick agreed that Loretta was fantastic; he knew her from the restaurant, she ate there often and Joseph was a good friend of his. He told me that he had been studying art at the University of Miami and Loretta had always encouraged him to pursue his talent.

When we finished our plates, Rick was kind enough to take them to the waiter across the room and bring us each a glass of champagne. He sat next to me and made a toast to new friends. We both smiled and as he sipped his champagne, I gulped mine. It took a few minutes, but the champagne had done its job and made my head light and carefree. I ran my hand up Rick's leg and stopped just short of his crotch. He then put his hand on my knee and kissed me once again on the neck and then on my cheek, then on my lips. I was so moved by his kisses that I let out a soft moan. His hand slowly moved up my thigh and then his fingers touched my clitoris, I moaned again, he slipped his finger into my vagina. By now my moans were becoming louder; Rick looked up to see if anyone was paying attention to us then he grabbed my hand and led me up the stairs to Loretta's office. Once inside he locked the door.

I was standing there in front of Loretta's desk looking around the room. It was a lovely office. It looked like Loretta. Very artsy; her favorite art was on every wall. A small mauve leather sofa against the west wall and two black leather chairs in front of her antique European pine desk. Her small desk chair was also black leather and I could picture her sitting there making decisions about art, artists, and how she was going to help them. The view from the window behind her desk was of the bay. At night, the view sparkled with the city lights. I could smell her perfume in the air and I sensed there had been sex in this office before.

Rick came up behind me and kissed my neck and pulled the zipper of my new acid green party dress down. The dress fell to the floor. I stepped out of it and he picked it up and carefully placed it over the back of one of the chairs. I was standing there in my black lace bra, matching panties, and black patent leather stiletto heels with the small acid green bows. Rick was watching me as he stepped out of his shoes, slipped out of his black jeans and pulled off his black polo shirt. His bronze body was as beautiful as I had imagined and the soft lights coming in the window from the street made it look even more beautiful.

He ran his hands over my ass and kissed me gently and then forcefully, I was breathing hard and could not wait for him to penetrate my very wet vagina. I pulled off my panties and tossed them on to Loretta's desk. Rick was strong enough to lift me up and penetrate me as he held me close to his warm body. It felt good to have my body wrapped around him and his gentle thrusts made me moan. He then rested my ass against the edge of Loretta's desk and moved in and out with more force, by then I was resisting the desire to scream out "Fuck me." I knew my voice would carry down into the gallery, so I held back. Just the same, I had a powerful orgasm and I wanted more. "Don't stop, don't stop" I whispered into the air. Rick leaned into me and muffled my words with his lips on mine.

Sex with Rick was wonderful and I did not want it to end. We both got dressed and went back down to the gallery. There was much excitement in the air in that room as well. Ken was a big success with the people that counted in Miami. He looked so handsome standing there accepting the praise in his shy way. John and Loretta were smiling and chatting with the guests and Joseph was busy writing down who was buying which painting. All I could think of was getting out of there so I could have more sex with Rick. I smiled at John and he smiled back and waved. He seemed oblivious to where I had disappeared to and I was glad about that. I grabbed another glass of champagne from the tray as it went by and held up the glass to Ken; he smiled, I gulped my champagne, as usual.

I don't know how many more glasses of champagne I had, but the next thing I knew was being in bed with Rick. I was naked, so was he. Rick was snoring, so I crawled out of bed and went into the bathroom. I turned on the light. My hair was a mess and my mascara was streaked down my face. I got in the shower.

By the time I stepped out of the tub, Rick was standing there looking at me with a towel in his hand and a big smile on his face. "Thanks" I said as I grabbed the towel and wrapped it around me. His beautiful face and bronze body still looked wonderful in the daylight and I was relieved to see him smiling. I knew I had been in a blackout, which meant anything could have happened. It must have been good.

Chapter 29

I was so happy to hear that John and Ken had decided to stay in Florida for another couple of weeks, which meant I could stay also. Ken invited John to go to Key West and Loretta said I could continue to stay at her house if I wanted to. I really wanted to stay because I really wanted to see Rick again.

He picked me up after the lunch shift the day Ken and John left for Key West and we took a drive along the beach. While we were driving he chatted on about his life, his friends, his dreams of becoming an artist and I just listened. I was not really interested in Rick as a person and I kept getting lost in my thoughts about Paul, Jon, Carlos, Mack, and the insanity of my earlier days in Miami and Ft. Lauderdale. We had dinner at a funky little dive in Hollywood and then went back to his place, which was the only thing I had really wanted to do from the beginning of the evening.

Rick went to the kitchen to get us some iced tea and by the time he came back, I was lying on the bed naked. He looked surprised but then he got that beautiful smile on his face as he stepped out of his shoes and sat on the edge of the bed. I ran my fingers up his thigh and rested my hand on his crotch. Just as I suspected, he was excited too. I moved my body closer to his and we started to kiss passionately. He yanked off his t-shirt and tugged desperately at his jeans till he finally pulled them off. His flesh was warm and the subtle fragrance of citrus filled my nostrils as I buried my face in his chest. I loved the way his strong arms held my small body so close to his and how he penetrated me with a gentle force, a force that I needed. We had sex on the bed, on the floor, against the dresser, on the sofa, in the kitchen, till our wet bodies could no longer move, the tile floor felt cool.

Rick and I saw each other for the next four nights, had sex, talked little – just the way I preferred it. By the end of the week, he did not call or return any of my three calls to him. I just sat near the pool, or in the pool, at Loretta's waiting to hear from him. I could not understand what had happened, why he did not call. Thoughts that he had met with a tragedy of some kind would dance through my head. Finally after sitting and moping for two days, I decided to go to the hotel and have a drink. I dressed in one of my sundresses and called a cab.

After a couple of days by the pool at Loretta's my skin had taken on a dark bronze glow. The white sundress looked striking against my skin and my hair was now strawberry blonde. My curls bounced up and down with each step as I walked across the pool deck towards the bar and sat down on a stool facing the restaurant. I ordered a soda water with lime and it wasn't long until I saw Rick through the window. I watched his strong arms as he carried the tray of food across the dining room and thought of how it felt to have them around me. I watched his gentile smile and thought of his sweet face looking at me as I came out of the shower that first morning. I watched his sexy lips and thought of how it felt when he kissed me passionately. Yes, I missed him, not as a person, but his sex, his touch, his passion.

I was so lost in my thoughts that I did not notice the attractive man who sat down next to me. I suddenly heard his voice, it startled me and I looked up. He had these amazing gray eyes and salt and pepper hair brushed back away from his face. He smiled and said "Good morning, beautiful." It made me blush. All I could manage was a sheepish smile. I suddenly felt naked as if he were reading my thoughts or that I said them out loud. He just sat there and waited for some kind of a response and when I did not speak, he decided to ask a direct question. "Are you staying here at the hotel?" "No" I said. My one word answer made him even more curious and it didn't look like he was going to give up. He introduced himself, "My name is Hank, I'm visiting from Boston, it sure is nice to be somewhere so warm, where the women are breathtaking and the drinks are luscious!" The drinks are luscious, I thought, is that the best you can do? I turned towards him with my whole body and put my hand out politely and said "The weather is breathtaking and the women are luscious," and we both broke into good belly laughs.

Hank was attractive, not as handsome as Rick, but I could tell he would make me laugh and take my mind off my obsession. I turned towards him on my stool and we started talking, at first about the hotel; Miami, Boston. We laughed, got serious, but mostly we enjoyed each other. He wasn't as old as his hair made him look and he was more than interesting. His job was to search out small companies that were not doing well and make an offer to buy them out if there was hope and then make recommendations as to how to make them profitable. He traveled a lot and he was single.

I don't know where the time had gone but the next thing I knew it was three o'clock in the afternoon. We had moved from the bar to a table in the shade and I was so comfortable talking to him that the time had just slipped by. I told him that I had to go, which was a lie, but I wanted to leave a bit of mystery. I had continued to drink only soda water as I did not want to continue on my usual path of self destruction. Hank invited me to dinner and I agreed to meet him in the lobby at eight o'clock that night. I remained the beautiful woman he met that day as I walked into the hotel lobby waving to him and watching him smile.

As I walked to the desk to ask for a cab, I felt a tap on my shoulder. I thought it was Hank and I turned with a big smile saying "Did you forget to tell me something?" But it was Rick, and he had a puzzled look on his face as he said "Yes, yes I did!" I'm sure he noticed my surprise. I got that sinking feeling in my stomach and that feeling of impending doom. I was sure whatever he was about to tell me was not what I wanted to hear. He took my arm and led me over to a more private area of the lobby, "I am sorry I did not call you back, I needed to think." He had such a serious look on his face, "I think, I feel, oh damn, you are too much." He turned and walked away, left me standing there. I remained in that spot until the concierge asked if he could help me with something. I asked for a cab.

When I got back to Loretta's, she was sitting in the shade on the patio reading the paper and drinking iced tea. She invited me to join her and offered me a glass of iced tea. I sat down. She told me that she had heard from Ken and that they would be back in a couple of days, they were really enjoying Key West. "That's wonderful" is all I could manage at that moment. "How about you, are you enjoying Miami Beach?" "Oh yes, it is so fabulous here." I said with absolutely no excitement. "Okay, what's going on?" asked Loretta. "Do you think I am too much?" I said in a sad voice. Loretta let out a big laugh and said, "It's our job to be too much, you just need to find the right people to be too much with!"

Chapter 30

As I dressed for my dinner date with Hank, I was thinking about what Loretta had said. Rick was probably just not the right person to be too much with. It was not the first time in my life I had heard that, there were so many men who told me that same thing in some way; were they all wrong, or were they just not capable of being with a woman who was too much?

I told myself that evening I would behave at dinner; try not to be too much, right away anyway. I thought Hank would be a "too much" kind of man who could handle a "too much" kind of woman. I had only hoped. He was very engaging and I looked forward to spending more time with him.

I could not decide what to wear – pants, skirt, dress? I heard Loretta's voice calling to me as she came up to the door of the guest house, "Darling do you want to have dinner with us tonight? We have plenty." I went to the front room in my bra and panties and told her that I had a date. "It must be with someone special, wearing great lingerie is a true sign!" I blushed and laughed. "I don't know what to wear, please help me decide." "Who is this date with?" Loretta asked. "A man I met today at the hotel, he is very charming, he makes me laugh, I think he can handle too much!" I joked. Loretta laughed. "Okay, the black silk Capri pants, black silk camisole, and I have the perfect denim jacket you can wear. Pull your hair back and wear your black sandals." "Which earrings should I wear?" I asked. "Get dressed and I will lend you a pair of mine." She said as she walked back out the door. A few minutes later she returned with a really nice denim jacket, short and very stylish with pretty silver buttons; and a pair of black and blue Australian crystal earrings. "You look very pretty; I hope this man appreciates true beauty." She said as she stepped behind me looking at my reflection in the mirror. "Thanks Loretta, I hope so too!" I said as I put a coat of red lipstick on my lips. "I'll call Carl to give you a ride to the hotel," she said, turning towards the door. I ran after her and gave her a big hug, "Thanks Loretta, you are the best."

Carl got me there right at eight and I saw Hank sitting in the lobby as the Mercedes pulled up. He looked so handsome in his periwinkle Polo shirt and his little boy smile. I hoped he did not know it was me arriving in such a fine car, but it was hard not to notice my red hair as Carl opened the door and helped from the back seat. I could see Hank get up and move quickly to the entrance to greet me. By the time Hank had reached me, Carl had driven away. Hank looked towards the Mercedes and then looked at me, smiled, and said "Wow, I didn't think it was possible but you look more beautiful than before." We stood there for a moment and then he said "I understand the food is very good at the hotel next door, you don't mind walking do you?" "No, walking will be good." I smiled. "Besides you have to make me laugh three times before we get there" I added. "You bet I will" Hank said as he took my hand in his and led me towards the sidewalk. On the way he stopped to pick a white gardenia and he put it in my hair.

Dinner was amazing and so was Hank; he had completely stolen my heart and he made me laugh. That evening I really got to be myself. Hank got to see my funny side and my serious side, my intelligence and my silliness; I felt close to him and I knew we would be friends. When we got back to the hotel, I had the bell captain call me a cab and as I got into the cab, Hank bent down and gave me the sweetest kiss. "Come have breakfast with me in the morning, eight thirty." I agreed, Hank shut the door and the driver moved the cab away from the curb and down the driveway towards Collins Avenue.

The next morning, Hank and I had breakfast and then he took me for a walk along the beach before leaving for a business meeting at noon. He asked if I would like to go for a drive to the West coast of Florida with him over the weekend. "We can leave on Friday afternoon and do some exploring along the way. I know of this wonderful Bed and Breakfast right on the beach. We have to take a boat to get there, you aren't afraid of the water are you?" He casually asked. "I am, but I know you will protect me" I said as I gripped his hand. He kissed me gently and told me he would call me later.

I decided to walk back to Loretta's house and do some window shopping on the way. I was happy, happier than I could remember. As I walked, I was thinking about how things seemed so wonderful now; how I was filled with feelings of contentment and joy; how I really did not want oblivion via the bottle or sex.

Chapter 31

On Friday afternoon, Hank picked me up at Loretta's and put my small suitcase in the trunk, opened the door for me and helped me into the car. He had borrowed a friend's Jaguar convertible for the weekend and he had the top down. It was a sunny spring day, very warm – the air was soft as it blew across my face and through my hair. Hank was wearing a white t-shirt and faded blue jeans and his body looked so fit. He was not his usual chatty self and neither was I. We both seemed to be enjoying the drive across Alligator Alley in the late afternoon sun. It was so quiet out there in the middle of the Ever-glades, only a few other cars passed us going towards Ft. Lauderdale.

Hank noticed a wide spot in the road along the water and we pulled over. "Do you think we will see any alligators?' he said with an excited little boy voice. "I hope not" I said as I moved close to him for protection. He held me tight and then we kissed, softly and then with an explosion of passion. It surprised me at first, but then I decided to just go with it. He kissed my neck and then moved his mouth down to my breast; his kisses felt wonderful and I was so excited. My hand was on his thigh and his hands were fumbling with my buttons. I decided to help and I unbuttoned my shirt exposing my naked breasts, and then pulled off my jeans and tossed them into the back seat. Hank did the same and pulled me up onto his lap. He penetrated me with such passion. His desire was moving and exciting and I felt the same fervor and urgency that he seemed to.

It was not long before I was moaning; his warm body was moving against mine and I could feel the sweat on my stomach and running down my back. My moans grew louder as our excitement intensified and they turned into a throaty "fuck me, fuck me" in Hank's ear. His body stiffened and his mouth searched for my lips, sweat was dripping from the tip of his nose and as his mouth met mine the drop of sweat moistened my lips. The salty taste exploded in my mouth and I pushed my tongue between his lips. The passion was so hot that I almost lost consciousness from hyperventilating. The car seat was restricting our movements and I felt like I was in bondage. I slowed down so that I could catch my breath and get myself in a better, freer position. I turned my body over and pulled myself up against the passenger door. Hank was able to position himself behind me and get into a rhythm that increased not only the pleasure but the amount of erotic language spewing from both our mouths. By the time Hank reached a climax, I had enjoyed at least three, sweat was dripping off both of us and the leather seat in his friend's Jaguar was a sticky mess. Hank managed to fall back into the driver's seat and I just laid against the door motionless for a long time.

We arrived in Naples just after seven and got something to eat at a restaurant near the marina. Hank then hired a boat to take us to the private island where we would stay. He was right – the Bed and Breakfast was gorgeous. The Shore Pine Inn was an old Cape Cod style home with three rooms upstairs that looked west towards the water. You could hear the waves lapping at the shore and the wind made a musical sound as it blew through the pines. By now, the sun had set and it was dark down on the beach except for the silver stream from the crescent moon up above and the star filled sky. Hank suggested we take a stroll along the shore before we showered and settled in for the evening. I loved the idea as it was such a beautiful evening and the sky was the most amazing star filled sky that I could remember ever seeing.

Our room was painted in a pale ice blue with honey colored oak floors. The furniture was Shaker style, simple but elegant. The bed, a four poster, was covered with a handmade quilt and lots of pillows. There was a small velvet love seat near the window and a small table with two chairs near the door. On each side of the bed there was a small table with a lamp and some books and along the wall by the closet was a dresser with a large mirror. The bathroom was completely white. An old claw foot bathtub sat against the far wall. The sink was also an antique and there were both a toilet and a bidet. Over the sink was a large antique mirror with an oak frame. In front of the sink and bathtub were fluffy blue rugs which stood out against the vintage white tile floor. There was an oak cabinet which held soft blue towels, handmade soaps and packages of bubble bath.

Hank opened his suitcase and placed his things in the dresser drawers and put his toiletries in the bathroom. I chose a package of lilac bubble bath and filled the tub with warm water. The fresh fragrance filled the room and I looked forward to settling in the warm water, the day's passionate sex was still on my body and my hair was sticky with the damp salt air. I stepped out of my clothes and slipped into the warm water and beckoned Hank to join me. The rest of the weekend was filled with erotic fiery sex and I knew it was just the beginning.

Chapter 32

Hank did make me laugh, more than three times, more than three hundred times before I agreed to move in with him. I had stayed on in Miami with him until his project there had been completed and then he dragged me to Dallas for his next conquest. Being in Miami with him was wonderful, I had Loretta to talk to and have lunch with, I had the gallery to visit and art to look at and of course I had Hank to make love to each day. He paid a lot of attention to me and I was the center of his world and he was the center of mine.

When we got to Dallas, I had no one but Hank. His company had provided us with a beautiful suite at a hotel right in the heart of the city, but I was alone most of the time.

At first I loved Dallas and all that it offered and most of all I loved Hank. With each passing day I would see less and less of him and I started to get lonely, discontented and very irritable. I had managed to control my drinking around Hank as I felt so filled up by his love. I was the center of his private world, but his business world took so much of his time and I was completely excluded from that except for the social dinners and parties. Hank never drank in the company of his colleagues and neither did I. For Hank I don't think it was an effort but for me it was torture. As time went on the constant smiling, polite chit chat and endless listening was wearing on my now fragile nerves. It seemed all too inevitable that I would sooner or later look for something to distract me.

Shopping did not fulfill me, neither did sightseeing, reading, or exercising; nothing seemed to fill the void in me anymore. I was lonely and bored. I walked through the streets aimlessly. I drove through the city with no destination. At times I could think of nothing but how much I loved Hank and then there were times when I was so angry at him it made me scream. I became the crazy screaming woman driving through Dallas with no destination and no hope.

On September fourteenth at ten twenty three in the morning I was on one of my aimless wanders when I was hit by a car whose driver had failed to come to a complete stop in time at the crosswalk I was occupying. I don't remember getting hit but I remember lying in the street wondering how I had gotten down there on the ground, then it all went black. The next thing I was aware of was a paramedic hooking me to an IV in the ambulance. By the time Hank arrived at the hospital, I had been treated for minor cuts and bruises and a bump on the head. The car did not hit me hard but my body was in shock from the impact and the doctor thought that I would probably be in some pain over the next few days and prescribed some Demerol.

Hank was as attentive as he could be and still do his job and I was happy just to lay in bed for a few days and sleep. The Demerol helped the pain and the boredom. By the end of the week I was back on my feet again and very restless. I went to the hotel restaurant to have lunch and decided a glass of wine sounded good. It was so good that I had three more, no lunch, and staggered back to the room and passed out. I think Hank came in about eleven and asked why I had not joined him for dinner as we had planned. "I was not feeling well" is all I could say. I said that to Hank a lot over the next couple of months. It was not long until I was drinking the way I had in the past. I even wondered how I had controlled it all that time.

John had stayed in contact and he knew something was wrong with me. One day he showed up at the hotel. He found me in the bar slumped to one side in an all too familiar position. He greeted me warmly and helped me off the bar stool and took me back up to my room. I was a mess. John knew it, Hank knew it, I knew it.

My past experience had showed me that I did not have to live this way but my present state of mind told me what's the use. John let me sleep that afternoon but never left my side. He knew that he was my only hope for not having to die this way. Hank had become so embarrassed of me and sick of finding me drunk in the bar that even though he loved me he easily let me go. John had packed my things and called a cab to take us to the airport. Rescued once again by my angel.

Chapter 33

Back at John's I had to make some tough decisions. Did I want to change and did I want his help. I felt like it wasn't worth it – the struggle, the pain, but deep inside I knew I did not want to die.

I also desperately wanted to be in love but I did not want anyone to get close. I wanted you to know who I was, but I knew if you did you would tell me to go away. I was scared, very scared. My fears ruled my life, but it was easier to escape them via the bottle than to face them and change. Was I still strong enough to control my drinking or did I get help, that was the big question.

John worked with a woman named Karen who had nine years of sobriety in AA and he invited her to the house to meet me. She was a lovely woman about my age who had a sparkle of life in her eyes. John sat with us for a few minutes and then excused himself after bringing us a pot of coffee and a plate of his delicious butter cookies.

Karen was a gentle woman and she shared a bit of her story with me and I immediately related to her. I was relieved to hear that I was not the only person on the planet that felt the way I did. She took me to some meetings and I listened to and identified with other people and made new friends. I was feeling stronger each day as I learned more and more about not drinking without having to control it all by myself. I had the love and support of so many wonderful people. After going to meetings for three months I was able to be of service in AA and got involved in conducting a weekly meeting at the woman's jail.

I did it for the next three years and it was an amazing experience. I can't say that I got anyone sober during the three years that I carried the message of hope to the woman in jail, but I was still sober three years later. Maybe I was just ready, maybe this stuff really works. The one important piece of evidence in my life was that it was the first time I had not found myself drunk, coming out of a blackout, or just plain sick from drinking in more than three years and that was good enough for me.

During those three years, I got a job working in an office and I decided to go back to school. I had no idea what I wanted so I just started taking general education classes. I loved school. I enjoyed the exchange of ideas and the new lines of thinking and my life got bigger and bigger. I had many new friends and of course John and Ken were both still a part of my life. John was still teaching at the University and Ken was still doing his art. They traveled in the summer and always invited me to join them wherever they would go. I had such a busy schedule it was not possible – which made me sad as I enjoyed their company so much.

After a year of night classes, I decided to get my degree in journalism. I had always loved to write and I was very curious about everything. It seemed like the right choice. So I continued on with my job during the day and two classes a quarter at night. My life was not perfect, it actually had a lot of challenges, but I was able to stand up to most of them in some way and get on with life. I had dated a few guys in AA and at school but I was too focused on my new life to get serious about any of them.

In December, we had to register for the upcoming quarter which would start in January. I had taken a few hours off from work to go and register for my two classes and there he was just standing there, tall, handsome, gray wool trousers, white oxford shirt open at the collar, half glasses resting on his nose. He looked up over the glasses at me with the most incredible blue eyes that just sparkled and he smiled. I smiled back. Inside I was moved in a way I had not paid much attention to for a long time. I was excited. I could feel the sensation in my thighs as I looked at him. I was speechless. I managed to get registered and leave the building but I could not stop thinking of his beautiful eyes and his brilliant smile. Once in the car, I reached between my legs and recalled the wonderful sensations of something I had denied myself for a long time. Those feelings were still there and apparently alive and well.

I had dinner that night with my friend Kathy at a small café that we both enjoyed, and we laughed about our crazy lives, work, school, family – the usual stuff. I told her about this man and it made me blush to talk about him. She teased me about it a little and told me to go for it. How could I go for it, I did not know who he was or whether I would ever see him again. Besides where would I fit him into my schedule? Kathy assured me that I would find the time. She had no idea who I was sexually and I had almost forgotten myself. But now the feelings were being aroused once again and it seemed like they had a life of their own. We finished dinner went to a meeting and then I went home. It was nice to have a few weeks with no school papers due, but it seemed like I had too much time for day dreaming. I decided to take a hot bath and read the trashy novel I had in the pile of books by my bed.

The next morning I woke with an obsessive need to see this man again. I had not had this intensity of feeling for a long time and it surprised me. I was feeling both anxious and sexual and I needed to do something about it. It was Friday and I had to get to work. I showered and washed my hair and chose my navy blue wool skirt and baby blue cashmere sweater. It took me longer than usual to get ready and I was almost late for work.

I ran out of my apartment and tripped over the planter by the door and cursed all the way to the car. I tore out of the parking lot and narrowly missed one of my neighbors walking her dog. Once on the freeway, I was driving like a maniac – weaving in and out of traffic, jumping from lane to lane, trying to get ahead of the already very heavy morning traffic all the way to my exit.

I almost arrived on time but I ran smack into a man on my way to the elevator when I was distracted by the security guard Jerry telling me good morning. The man lost his grip on his cup of coffee, and the coffee spilled down the front of my sweater. The heat of the coffee shocked me and it didn't take long for it to soak through my bra to my skin. I was so stunned it just stopped me in my tracks; it stopped him too, as the paper cup hit the floor at our feet. He immediately pulled a white cotton handkerchief from his pocket and dabbed at the coffee on my breasts.

Oh how embarrassing, this is just too much I thought. I raised my hands to my chest reaching for the handkerchief and I said "It's okay, I'll get it!" He blushed and agreed that was probably a better idea. He had a great smile and an adorable dimple. I apologized and he said "No, it was really my fault, I got distracted by your beauty and got in the way. Please let me pay for the sweater and take you next door to get something else to wear." "I don't think they are open yet." I said. "Yes, you are probably right. I can't let you go off to the office like that though. I am staying just across the street – let me get you one of my shirts," he said politely. "I'm with Talbert and Associates, the Philadelphia office, I came to help one of the attorneys with a tough case he has." I thought for a moment and then said "If you can wait a couple of minutes for me to explain to my boss, I'll go across the street with you." I went to my office but my boss, Mr. Katz, was out sick so I let the receptionist know that I would be back in a while as I had had an accident. Julie noticed the terrible stain on my sweater and made a sad face,

"Such a great sweater too!" "I know – it's one of my favorites, I hope the stain comes out." I walked out.

Once on the elevator I had a moment to think about the situation, the handsome man wiping at my breasts, his dimple, his gentle voice, my sexual angst; by the time the elevator doors opened to the lobby I was breaking into a slight sweat. He was standing there facing the elevator looking a little awkward in his navy pinstripe Brooks Brothers' suit, white dress shirt and pale yellow silk tie.

He took my arm gently and escorted me from the building. We crossed the busy street to the hotel and took the elevator to the tenth floor. We walked down the long hallway to room 1069. I noticed the number and it made me smile. He did not notice though. Once inside the room he went to the closet to get me a shirt and I stood near the door and looked around. He seemed to be a pretty meticulous guy. Everything was neat and orderly, as if he were not really staying there, just the way I liked my room too! This also made me smile and I was getting that warm feeling again. Actually I was feeling hot and I was trying to control it. He handed me a perfectly pressed light blue shirt and I walked towards the bathroom.

I slipped out of my sweater and noticed that my bra was stained as well. I took it off and ran it under some cold water to see if I could get the stain off. I looked in the mirror and I could see his reflection looking at mine. I paused and then put my attention back on the stained bra. It looked as though the stain had completely come out of my bra and I reached for a towel to dab it dry when I felt his hand brush my hair back away from my neck and he put his lips ever so softly on my neck giving me a delicate kiss. I was not surprised and I did not want him to stop. He kissed the top of my back between my shoulder blades and then he ran his tongue down my spine. I felt my body relax and the towel and bra fell to the floor as I turned my body towards him and kissed his lips as gently as he kissed my neck.

He responded with a more passionate grip around my waist and more pressure on my mouth. We kissed fervently and I could feel the wetness between my legs and the heat rising in my body. I could feel his excitement as well. He lifted me on to the counter and pushed my skirt up exposing the tops my thigh high stockings then saw that I was not wearing any panties. This got him more excited and he dropped his suit jacket to the floor, loosened his tie – pulling it over his head to remove it, unbuttoned his shirt and dropped it to the floor as well. Kneeling down in front of me he put his hands on the inside of my thighs, gently separating my legs to expose my now very wet labia. I gasped, he moaned. His mouth moved towards my spread thighs, my head was clouded with excitement and all I wanted was for him not to stop.

After a few minutes, he picked me up and carried me to the bed while kicking off his shoes. He laid me on the bed and unbuttoned his pants while I wiggled out of my skirt. He dropped his pants to his ankles and then stepped out of them leaving them to wrinkle on the floor. I was lying there in nothing but my thigh high stockings and black heels, my body stimulated with excitement from his touch and his kisses. Finally he pulled off his boxers, exposing a ferocious hard on. He knelt between my spread legs and looked into my eyes. I watched him as he pulled me up towards him and let our bodies touch. Our skin seemed to be electrically charged and it felt amazing to be touched. It had been so long since I let anyone get close to me in this way and I had forgotten how much I not only liked it but how much I needed it.

Oblivion would soon be mine. I could feel the sexual animal in me rising.

I wrapped my legs around his waist and invited him to penetrate me. He moved in and out with long gentle strokes, feeling every square inch of my throbbing wet vagina. I was panting and gasping with pleasure at every stroke. The all too familiar sexual junkie had emerged and I knew I was not going back to the office for a while. His strokes became faster and more passionate till he pulled away from me to keep from finishing too quickly. He rolled over on his back moaning and panting trying to recover while I was trying to figure out where he had gone. His breathing calmed and I grew more anxious so I flipped myself to my knees next to him and buried my face in his chest, he smelled so good even though his skin was wet with sweat. I could feel his heart pounding and I could see he was still good to go for more so I climbed on and took the lead. It wasn't long till he was once again moaning and I was screaming.

We changed positions several more times before finishing in a heap on the floor next to his clothes, hair wet with sweat and bodies twisted together. I don't know how much time had passed before I was finally able to get up and into the shower. He followed. The warm water felt good running over me and my head started to clear from the mood altering fog that had developed from having sex with this beautiful stranger. I felt good, too good to go back to the office.

I wanted more. I wanted more.

He was true to his word. When I was at the office the next day, a gift from Neiman Marcus containing a very pretty baby blue cashmere sweater and a note with the words "Thank you" arrived. I did not see him again before he went back to Philadelphia but I did not stop thinking about him for a long, long time.

Chapter 34

The hardest part of my sweater encounter was that it set in motion the long forgotten desires in me, the desires I replaced with school, work, and meetings. I had forgotten how much I desired to be desired. I had forgotten to notice the way men looked at me, I had forgotten how much I had shut myself off from that part of me and how painful it was to be wanting, needing, and yet not participate in it.

Weeks had passed and I was feeling more and more agitated at work and at school. I was feeling tired yet restless. I did not want to get up in the morning and I had to force myself to get out to work. I knew it was time for something new, but what? A new job, a new place to live, a new life! I wanted more, more of something, I didn't know what – but something.

One day, I decided I needed a new adventure and some spontaneity in my life so I made the decision to move to Seattle. I had a cousin there and he seemed to think that I would have no trouble fitting in with the culture there and he would let me stay with his family till I got my own life. It was exciting planning the move to a new place and after all, I had all my friends in AA that I had not met yet. The hardest part of moving was letting go of everything I already knew and had. I could only hope that I would be able to replace it all with better things. What I know today is that if I am meant to be somewhere, it all gets better and better.

All my friends were so great. They shipped me off with love and support and lots of parties. John and Ken were especially wonderful; they hired some people to help me pack the small truck for my big move. The trip across the country was beautiful, it was late spring and everything seemed so beautiful and new. I had never done anything this bold before and as scared as I was, I was also excited and elated that I could do such a brave thing alone and I knew it would make me grow.

At the end of the first long driving day, I stopped for the night and checked into a motel. I got the telephone book out and called AA to see if there was a meeting that night nearby. I spoke to a woman on the phone who made me feel welcomed and who said she would send someone to pick me up for the seven thirty meeting. It was six fifteen so I told her I would be in the coffee shop next door having some dinner.

Sure enough, just as she promised a woman, Shirley, showed up to take me to the meeting. She was great. She made me laugh all the way to the meeting. The wonderful thing about people in AA is that immediate connection we have to each other; that knowledge that we are never alone. Shirley introduced me to everyone, and I mean everyone. It was good that we got there early. After the meeting a group got together for ice cream and they took me along. We talked and laughed and had a wonderful time till I could no longer hold my eyes open. Shirley dropped me off at the motel, wished me luck and told me to keep coming back. It made me smile and I knew I always had a home in AA.

On the second night, I was not as lucky, there was no meeting in the small town I stopped in. It was okay though, I was tired. I got something to eat at the diner and went to bed. The next morning, I got on the road before the sun came up. It was a beautiful day too, the Rocky Mountains lay just ahead and I was looking forward to driving over them. I had never seen them before and they took my breath away. The early morning sun cast a beautiful light on them. The highway took me right through Denver and the excitement of the big city. I stopped for gas on the west side of the city and chatted with some nice people from New Zealand doing a six month tour of the United States. They told me about some of the things they had seen and how much they looked forward to all that the West offered. Yellowstone, the Grand Canyon, Zion, Bryce, the Painted Desert, the Pacific Ocean, yes, we do have a wonderful country full of so much exquisite beauty. I too wanted to see it all and I knew I would eventually.

Five days it took me to get to Seattle, five days full of incredible beauty, interesting people and my wandering mind. I had lots of time to reflect on my life and lots of time to be grateful that I had come so far from those days on the bar stool at Blues. How lucky was I that I had survived my own self destructive impulses and behavior to be here now embarking on a new life.

My cousin, Rob, and his wife Susan, welcomed me and made me feel at home but I knew it was important to get my own place as soon as possible. I started looking for a job and a place the very next day and without too much effort landed a job at a gourmet grocery store. It was located not too far from the college I wanted to attend and it paid well. I was also able to find a room for rent in a lovely home in a safe neighborhood that reminded me of living at Helga's. I had a big bedroom and my own bathroom. I had to share the kitchen and the front entrance but there was a small balcony off my second floor bedroom that I enjoyed. The woman who owned the house had been divorced for seven years and she told me that she got lonely in the house by herself. Her name was Maureen and we became the best of friends in a short time.

Chapter 35

It was summer now and the days were long and I was settling into my new life, working hard, getting to know the city, making new friends. Life was good. I was feeling good too; I was walking each day and eating well thanks to my job, and getting to plenty of meetings. They were different in Seattle but very good and I seemed to be staying on track.

On Wednesday evenings, I attended a group regularly and became friends with a very pretty woman named Karla. Her boyfriend, Sean, was the secretary of the meeting so she was always there. She called me regularly and on my day off I usually joined her for lunch.

On the Fourth of July, Sean organized a big party at his house and Karla asked me to come. I had to work early that day but I promised Karla I would come by when I got off. By the time I arrived, the party was in full swing.

There were lots of food, volleyball, and great music. People were dancing and having a good time. I knew some of the guests but there were lots of people I did not know. I was shy at first; it seemed like it had been a long time since I had attended a party with so many people.

In every social event there are always those few who draw you in and make you feel comfortable and it was no different this time. Debbie and Mike were the instigators at Sean's party; they made everyone laugh and made sure there was lots of fun to go around. I liked both of them immediately and let them pull me into the fun.

They orchestrated a game that included joining together everyone who was playing by a string. They managed to talk about twenty people into playing along with them. The rules were simple; you had to put the string down your pant leg and then hand the end to the next person. It was funny and we all laughed way too hard. I could hardly stand up I was laughing so hard. The man who was next to me, James, was making me laugh too. He had a wonderfully sardonic wit. At the end of the game, he invited me outside for some air. On the way out the door I grabbed a cold drink for each of us and we sat on the porch stairs.

The sun was setting and it would soon be time for the fireworks. Many people left but a few of us decided to walk down to the lake to watch the fireworks. It was about a mile and the night air felt good. James and I walked together and talked about the day, Seattle, work – the usual stuff. When we got to the lake, we all found seats at the edge of the dock where the boats were tied up. There were lots of people there, laughing, having fun. Children were running around with sparklers. It was great. I was great. James was great.

About half way through the fireworks show, I felt James' lips softly caress the back of my neck, a feeling of excitement shot down my spine. I had not given into this feeling in a while and it surprised me. I wanted to move away and yet I didn't. I let him kiss me again on the neck, I could feel my nipples get hard, my head relaxed and then I felt his lips on mine. I gave into his lips and kissed him back. We finished watching the fireworks and then walked quietly all the way back to Sean's. As I said good night to him he asked if he could see me again. The following day was my day off and I agreed to get together with him in the morning for breakfast.

James – tall, thin, good looking, moved me in a way I had not experienced before. His long dark brown hair hung loose around his unshaven face. He was not the kind of man I would normally be attracted to. He had relocated to Seattle from Newark, NJ, and had a thick East coast accent. His voice was deep and he said everything with great drama and color. I had not had this much fun in a long time.

I imagined his sex would be the same way, dramatic and colorful. The thought of it thrilled me.

After breakfast, he took me to his apartment which was downtown near Pike Street Market overlooking the Puget Sound. It was a large studio full of light. The focal point of the room was a beautiful antique wrought iron bed that was strategically placed in front of the large window that looked west towards the water. I remember feeling excited as I got lost for a moment in the thought of being naked and tied to the bed.

James took off his jean jacket and tossed it over the back of the desk chair as he passed by on his way to the kitchen to get a glass of water. He placed the glass of water on the table next to the bed and pulled the covers back exposing the soft yellow sheets. I was still standing in the same spot watching him move around the bed. The fact that he assumed we would have sex thrilled and scared me at the same time. I had always found that those two emotions seemed to wrap around each other for me and add to the excitement of sexual adventure. My stomach had butterflies and I could feel the flush of passion shoot down my legs. I closed my eyes and felt the warm rush of desire fill my chest.

James came up behind me and kissed me on the neck as he slid my jacket off my shoulders and pulled it away from my arms. My body relaxed and I fell back against his firm body as my jacket fell to the floor. He then reached around my trembling body and lifted up my skirt exposing my lace panties. He slipped his warm hand down into my panties past my abdomen and flicked his fingers through the soft pubic hair below. The excitement was so powerful that my knees went weak and I had to lean forward and grip the iron bed for support. As I leaned forward James knelt down behind me and kissed me softly on my ass. By now I was moaning with pleasure and excitement – my eyes closed and I slipped into oblivion. He ran his hands down my bare legs and pulled off my shoes and socks. He then picked up my now limp body and laid me on the bed with my legs hanging over the edge. My body tingled with excitement as I watched him pull off his shirt and pants exposing his tattooed body and raging hard on.

James pushed my skirt up around my waist and ripped my panties off my body; I screamed in ecstasy. He then put my legs up on his shoulders and penetrated me with urgency. With each thrust I moaned and screamed "Fuck me." And fuck me he did; in every way possible. The wrought iron bed served us well that day. I think we had needed it more than either of us knew. I stayed with him all day and night and by the next morning he was serving me breakfast in bed.

I didn't want to leave but it was a work day for me and I was already late. I called my boss and said my car had a flat tire. James told me he would call me later so we could get together for dinner. He called me as he promised and we got together that night for dinner and sex. For the next three weeks we had almost non stop sex in every available moment of each day. It was wonderful, it was addictive. The more I got, the more I wanted. I did not want to talk or go anywhere – all I wanted was sex.

I started making up new late excuses and my boss was starting to wonder what was wrong with me. I was feeling crazy too. I could hardly keep my mind on my work – all I could think about was James and our sex.

After three weeks James picked me up after work and took me to dinner in a nearby restaurant. I didn't really want to eat but he insisted. I felt his tension and wondered why he was acting so strange. He told me he had to stop seeing me. My jaw dropped; I sat there motionless. Why, why was he telling me this? What had I done? I wanted to beg and plead but I couldn't. He said it was all too much for him and he had to stop. Memories of Rick and others flowed back into me and I felt sick to my stomach. I excused myself and left the restaurant. I walked back to the store, got in my car and drove home. I sat on the floor of my room and sobbed for what seemed like hours; finally Maureen knocked on the door and asked if I was okay. I told her I had a tough day at work and that I was just getting out some pent up frustrations. I then wiped my eyes and got in the shower.

Chapter 36

I stuffed my feelings deep down in my heart and went back to my life. I started flirting with every attractive man who came across my path. During the next month over a dozen men picked me up for a date; all of whom I had sex with at least once. The huge hole in my soul had returned and none of the sex, desire or attention could begin to fill it up; it just got bigger. Maureen noticed and tried to talk to me but I just shut her out. She looked at me with such sadness but left me alone.

One night I had picked up a man who said he was in town on business and was staying at a nearby hotel. He seemed nice and he was very good looking and very sexy. I went with him back to his hotel and we had sex – crazy sex, animal sex – I just didn't care anymore. I just wanted to not feel. As I lay there sweating and exhausted I realized that I did feel, that I could not make feeling go away with the sex; it was like the drinking – one was too much and a thousand was not enough. What was I doing? Was I crazy? I got up and started to dress and he stopped me. "You're not going anywhere till I say it's time to go." He said to me in a low mean voice. I jerked my arm away from his grip and said "I'm leaving, I need to go." He grabbed me harder and threw me back on the bed. I protested for a moment and then got afraid, so I just gave in. The following two hours were some of the scariest that I could remember, I felt like a prisoner and everything was out of control. He finally went into the bathroom and I grabbed my clothes and slipped out the door. I was lucky no one was in the hall and I managed to get to the elevator and dress on my way to the lobby. I ran away from the hotel. It was early in the morning and still a little dark; I saw a gas station and went to the phone booth there and called Karla.

Karla did not know what was wrong as she could not understand what I was saying between sobs except that I was at this gas station and I needed her help; she came to my rescue right away, no questions asked. It took her about fifteen minutes to reach me as I stood by the phone booth and shivered in the cool early morning air, sobbing. I had no idea how I had gotten so far out of control. The whole situation was symbolic of what my life had become; I was a prisoner of my own obsession. The obsession to not feel my emotions and escape the loneliness and despair that I had created.

The pain was deep and I could hear the eerie sound of the wind blowing through the hole in my soul again and I was granted the opportunity to heal my life again; it was my choice. Could I choose recovery?

Karla took me to her place and I got cleaned up and we talked for a long time. She told me that she was concerned about my well being and suggested I get some professional help. I wished I could tell her that I agreed I needed it; but my thinking was that I could control it. I just had to try harder. She did not let me out of her sight for the next few days and on Tuesday night she took me to a support group where she thought I could get some help.

I was not ready to embrace the idea with an open mind and an open heart; I simply kicked and screamed "why me!" a lot during those next few months. I could not see that I used my need for sex to change the way I felt about other things in my life. It did not take long until I was finding excuses as to why I didn't need those meetings anymore and I never made the decision to get professional help, either.

As the months dragged on, my life continued to spin out of control and I had to keep it a secret. I would show up for work but I could no longer stay focused on the tasks at hand and constantly slipped into deep thoughts of fantasy and imagined sexual excursions. In my emotional life my closeness to others was becoming more difficult and my friendships started to slip away. The only two people who never gave up on me were Maureen and Karla. I would constantly push them away but they would not give up on me. They were true angels, just like John had been. None of them ever doubted my value as a human being even though I did. I knew I was a useless piece of shit and it would never be different for me; I had lost all hope.

By the following March my life had become so small; smaller than it had been in a long time. I would show up at work and then go home to my lonely room where I would masturbate to try to push down the feelings of my loneliness. I was in a constant state of agitation and the thought of picking up a drink was with me daily. I had learned a lot about my alcoholism and I knew a drink would not solve anything but I could not stop thinking about it.

When I was on the freeway in the morning going to work, thoughts of dying filled my brain. When would the pain and the loneliness end? One day Karla came by the store as I was walking out and insisted I get in her car. She was always so pushy and I had no excuse not to. She took me to get some coffee and we talked. Well, she talked and – I broke down and cried. I finally let down my defenses and told her of my loneliness and despair. She comforted me and assured me that there was hope; I just needed to find it once again.

Chapter 37

By May I did find that hope at an AA meeting of all places. It came in the form of a man named Louis.

Louis was a very handsome man, twelve years older than me. He had a radiant smile and a lot of self confidence. He reminded me of Jack. He was so charming. Louis happened to sit next to me at the Saturday night speaker meeting. It was birthday night and he was celebrating ten years of sobriety. I had celebrated six years back in November and in spite of all I had been through I managed to hang on to my six years. We chatted briefly before the meeting started and after the meeting ended he asked if I would like to go for a ride with him on his Harley. I said yes and gave Louis my telephone number.

Several weeks had passed before we actually went for that ride. It had been many years since I had climbed on the back of a motorcycle and thoughts of Jeff and Alberto came to mind and made me smile. We had a fun day together and when he dropped me back at home he asked if he could take me to dinner and a meeting the next week; I agreed that it would be fun, so we did. We went out for several weeks and I was feeling quite infatuated with him. He was funny and delightful and we really enjoyed each other a lot.

One Saturday night he took me to dinner and as usual we had a wonderful time, he had a knack for telling stories that would make me laugh. This night was different though, we both felt it, the desire to be more than friends, the time to be sexual had arrived. I knew it by the way he leaned towards me as he talked, by the way he touched my hand, by the way he would get that little boy smile as he would blush. Yes he was ready and so was I.

He invited me to his home that night. I was a little nervous; I had not had sex in a while. Of course I told myself that it was different this time that I had been in control for a while now and I had self knowledge; I was cured.

As we pulled up to the house the sun was setting but it was still light enough to see the house and the yard. The house was a very nice white split level with dark green trim. The yard was immaculate; the grass was mowed and the shrubs were trimmed and there were several large trees next to the garage. Louis pulled the bike up the driveway and jumped off to open the garage door. It was a big garage, big enough for two cars and his Harley. He parked the bike in the garage next to his truck and I got off and looked around for a moment. Lots of tools lined the walls and filled the shelves. In front of his truck there was the lawn mower, shovel, rake, and garden saw. It was all so organized. I was impressed.

He took my hand and led me out of the garage up the walkway and unlocked the front door. There were six stairs up to the main floor level and six down to the bottom level. He took me upstairs and gave me a tour of the house. The entire upstairs had dark wood floors with area rugs and a navy blue leather sofa and matching love seat set in an L configuration that took up the majority of the living room. A large square oak coffee table, two matching end tables and a television filled the rest of the room leaving very little space for moving around. There was a large picture window over the sofa which faced west and I could see remnants of the pink sunset sky between the large evergreen trees.

Attached to the living room was the dining room with a large table set against the wall and four chairs. There was a sliding glass door off the dining room which led to a wooden deck which was covered with pots of colorful flowers. There were steps which led down to a big back yard which was also perfect. The kitchen had a large window over the sink that looked out to the back yard which faced east and I imagined the morning light filling the room. The kitchen had oak floors with laminate counter tops and matching oak trim. It looked like the kitchen of a man who liked to cook.

He then led me to the back of the house where the master bedroom and bathroom were. The bathroom was very masculine and I could smell the scent of sandalwood soap in the air. His bedroom was also very masculine, oak furniture with simple lines and a king size bed with a chocolate brown comforter on it. The room was quite large and there was an area just inside the door for his desk and computer. Then he took me downstairs where the furniture was worn and looked very comfortable, another television and a sliding glass door which led out to another wooden deck. There were two guest bedrooms in the down-stairs area and a small bathroom.

At the end of the tour we went back upstairs to the living room. Louis invited me sit down on the sofa. He then went to the kitchen and got us each an ice tea. He sat down next to me and we talked about the house and he told me of some plans that he had for fixing up the place. Then there was an awkward silence. This was quite strange for us as we usually had lots to say to each other. I felt his nervousness and I am sure he felt mine.

Louis finally reached over and kissed me on the lips, I kissed him back. His lips were soft and warm and very inviting. My body relaxed and I leaned back on the sofa. Louis moved with me and placed a tender kiss on my neck, I felt my nipples stiffen. I was very receptive to his continued kisses on my neck as I pulled him close to me. With each kiss the heat rose till Louis finally pulled me up off the sofa by my hand and led me back into his bedroom. I pulled off my jeans and t-shirt and leaped on to his bed. He followed me there kissing my neck, breasts, stomach, thighs, oh my, I was now moaning in ecstasy. Not only did I want Louis but I wanted him to want me with all the passion he had. I was so hot I could hardly catch my breath; I was fighting the urge to slip into an altered state. I really liked Louis and I wanted to remain present. I was distracted by my desire to stay with my feelings and I missed my first attempt at orgasm. Louis finally got naked and slipped into me with gentle sweet strokes. As his passion rose, so did his moans and the ferocity of his strokes. It did not take long until we were both screaming in ecstasy; orgasm had arrived for both of us. Louis held me close to him for a few minutes and then he finally rolled over on his back releasing his grip. I could feel the coolness of the air as it hit my damp body; I shivered and pulled the comforter over me. I rolled on to my side so I could see Louis laying there, his breathing was returning to normal. He was a handsome man. His face was tan from the sun and it was striking against his wavy silver hair. His arms were strong from the work that he did and his legs were strong from riding the motorcycle. I reached over and ran my fingers over his chest and down his arms; he smiled a beautiful smile, a peaceful, joyful smile.

The weeks that followed that night were filled with happiness and a lot of sex. I would go to work each day and think of nothing but Louis. My mind raced and my body tingled with excitement as I would recall each previous night's events and I would have to go to the ladies room and touch myself to calm them. I was crazy about Louis and after a short time I moved into his house. I had never been in love and I had never wanted to be with anyone as much as I wanted to be with Louis; not even Paul.

Chapter 38

My relationship with Louis took on substance and strength and we spent a lot of time together. That first summer he took me on many weekend motorcycle trips. It was a different lifestyle for me and I was not sure I really liked all of his friends but we had fun and I was sure I was in love and that's all that mattered for me. Yes, life was fabulous and so were me and Louis.

After we lived together for four years Louis decided we should get married. I was vacillating as I had a really big fear of committing at that level. I had always been a free spirit and even though I had been faithfully living with Louis I was scared. After much thought and discussion with Karla I decided to go forward and marry Louis. We had a small ceremony on a Friday afternoon and then went on a four day trip to the San Juan Islands.

During the four years previous to our marriage we had our ups and downs and the usual relationship bumps but for the most part we were happy. Being married seemed to change everything. It was different after the wedding and I know that I was the one that started to change. It seemed as though I felt trapped and ordinary; I started to live my mother's life and I was definitely not ready for it.

I decided to pursue my journalism career and secured a position at the Eastside Journal writing a daily column. Louis continued his career with only a few more years till he could retire. We spent a lot of time talking about and doing research on where we would move after he retired. In the summer we would take long trips to the Southwest in search of a warm dry place.

After another two years together and a major move to a new city the excitement of new love had worn thin and we were just another couple, going to work, cooking dinner, watching television, going to bed so we could get up and do it all over again. We had lost our spark. I had intimacy issues. We had lost the passion.

The new city was small and I missed the excitement of Seattle and my job at the Eastside Journal. I was now writing a bi-weekly column for a small local newspaper which was full of heartwarming stories of the countless generations of cattle ranchers and farmers. I started to get depressed. Louis was becoming increasingly grumpy because he too missed Seattle and all the friends he had left behind.

After another year passed Louis did finally settle into our new life. He liked the peace and quiet and the nice weather California had to offer. I did like the weather and our beautiful home on thirty acres of oak covered land and our three dogs but I still missed the excitement of the city. I spent a lot of time wandering around the property with the dogs and working in the garden but nothing felt like enough. I was restless. I needed more.

I started to eat.

As I put on the pounds I became more distant from Louis and he became more distant from me. We no longer had sex like a couple in love. It was strained and difficult and I think Louis could no longer bear what I had become so he started sleeping on the couch and I slept alone in the bed. My existence was lonely and I was afraid and angry most of the time.

Louis became critical of me and I could not do anything right. As time passed I got used to his criticism and I no longer cared, I just collapsed into it and the incredible emptiness of my soul became unbearable.

The people that I worked with kept their distance as they never knew when I would snap. My Editor called me into his office on two occasions to say that he could no longer count on me for being a team player. On the third visit to his office he said that I would have to do something about my irritable nature or he would have to ask me to leave. This got my attention and I went home that night and asked Louis to go to counseling with me. "It doesn't work, I've done it before, it just doesn't work." He said, "and besides this is your problem not mine." I felt so sad, alone and flawed.

That night the despair was more than I could bear and I decided I just wanted to die. I sobbed and sobbed and then I called Karla, and as usual, she gave me her full attention and then she gave me her advice. "Honey, if he doesn't want to go that doesn't mean you can't go!" She said in a confident tone. She was right. If he didn't want to get help it did not mean that I had to suffer any longer. The next day I made an appointment with a woman named Ruth.

Chapter 39

Ruth was a small thin woman who had a Master's degree in Social Work which she received from the University of California. Short blonde hair framed her oval face and her olive skin suggested she was not a true blonde. She had dark brown intense eyes which seemed to penetrate my soul. She had a soft but authoritative voice which made me squirm when she asked me to tell her the truth. She dressed very casually, blue jeans, loose shirts and cowboy boots were her usual attire. Her office was in a small vintage house just outside of town that reminded me of the warmth and comfort of John's house.

During our first session we planned our strategy for what I wanted to accomplish during my weekly visits with her. I was so shut down around my feelings that it took almost the entire hour to get to it; I finally decided that I wanted to feel better about myself.

Ruth agreed that self esteem was a good beginning. And a beginning it was. It actually took over a year of weekly visits before I felt good about who I was.

During that year I started to grow up emotionally and take responsibility for my own feelings and actions. I also started to work out and I lost nearly twenty pounds in three months. Each week she would give me an assignment; sometimes it would be something as simple as repeating positive affirmations like, "I am smart and capable" to things that were far more difficult like letting Louis do his own things and stay out of his business.

Ruth encouraged me to get a new job that would pay more and let me express my intelligence. She also gave me the tools to find myself and to pursue the things that made me feel good. I started to feel wonderful and I also started to look wonderful too. My new weight loss and my firm muscles gave me the confidence to wear clothes that showed off my body like I did when I was young. I often thought about the days of shopping with Sheila and Loretta and all the fun clothes I use to wear.

I got a job writing a weekly column for The San Francisco Chronicle. I had to travel to San Francisco once a week which was fun and life was starting to look good again. The life came back to my eyes and to my soul. I started to laugh again and my heart felt so much lighter.

Louis constantly tried to engage me in his life but I could no longer sit around night after night watching television and having political arguments that I could never win no matter which side I was on. I set up a quiet room in the house where I could read and write which Luis objected to because in that room he was not part of my life.

In spite of the distance between us we would ride together on the weekends and we still went out to dinner with friends. I am sure most of our close friends felt the strain between us. I was all too aware of the strain myself and it was wearing me out.

Ruth did ask that I try to work on things with Louis because she knew how much I really did care for him; and how much I loved him. I told her that I did love him, but I was not sure whether I was actually capable of that emotion. There were so many things I was not sure of, and I had never told the truth about. I did not know what the truth was. I kept so many secrets even from myself that getting to the truth was difficult at best and nearly impossible in some cases.

Chapter 40

One weekend I invited Louis to join me at a very romantic hotel in the city. I had made all the arrangements for the room and the dinner. I told him I had to do some work and asked him to meet me in the restaurant at 7:30 PM.

When he arrived the Maitre de showed him to the table by the window that I had picked out and served him a coffee just as I had planned. I made him wait there for me for ten minutes and then I showed up in a very suggestive outfit. I had on a very short black leather skirt, a black lace camisole with a red leather jacket and red heels that clicked as I walked sexily across the wooden floor of the main dining room. Every eye in the room was on me as I moved towards Louis.

He smiled as he saw me coming towards him and stood up when I reached the table. The waiter was already there and pulled the chair away from the table so I could sit down and placed the white linen napkin across my lap.

"Wow, you look great! Louis said as he reached across the table to take my hand. His hand was warm and moist and it felt good to be touched by him. I did miss him. I did want him to want me and I so much wanted to desire him again. I closed my eyes for a moment to remember how I felt in the beginning with him; when our desire was new. A feeling of excitement shot down my legs and I knew there was something still alive between us.

We tried to keep the conversation light, leaving little room for criticism or emotions. Louis told me about the new motorcycle he wanted to buy and we talked about me learning how to ride my own motorcycle.

We enjoyed a lovely dinner of oysters on the half shell, tossed salad of baby greens, baked salmon and crème Brule for dessert. It was a wonderful meal.

After dinner we took a long walk through the city streets laughing about the early days of our relationship and all the wonderful places we had traveled together. Life felt good, I felt good, Louis' touch felt good.

When we arrived back at the hotel we kissed passionately in the elevator on our way up to the twenty third floor. By the time the elevator doors opened my jacket was off and Louis was pulling me towards our room. He was nearly in a sprint by the time we arrived in front of the door and we could not get the key to work because we were laughing which only made us laugh even more. By the time we got inside my stomach was aching and I had to pee. When I came out of the bathroom Louis was already laying on the bed naked waiting for me.

I turned on some music and very sexily slid out of my leather skirt. I stood in front of Louis in nothing but my thigh high stockings, black lace camisole and my red high heels. I moved my hips to the music and danced around the bed. Louis watched anxiously rolling over on to his stomach at the edge of the bed and when I got close to him he grabbed my hips and pulled me towards him burying his face in my crotch. I squealed with excitement. Maybe things were not over between us; maybe this was a new beginning. I loved the feel of Louis' warm flesh against mine, I missed him so much.

Louis rolled over on to his back and I knelt between his legs and pleasured him with my mouth, making delicious slurping sounds as he moaned. I moved my body over him and sat on his penis, the penetration made me scream and I rotated my hips till I came with a thundering shudder as I collapsed against his chest. He moved on to his side and thrust into me the way I liked it as I screamed in ecstasy, "fuck me, fuck me."

Chapter 41

I wish I could tell you that after that weekend we lived happily ever after but we did not. I could not keep Louis happy no matter how hard I tried and he could not get me to settle into his lifestyle. I made a decision to move away from the ranch and rented a small house in town about eight miles away.

I packed my personal belongings and the furniture from the guest room and left. I wanted him to ask me not to leave but he didn't even flinch when I walked out the door. It was one of the saddest days of my life.

The town we lived in was small and we had many mutual friends so we did continue to see each other and neither of us would give up the AA meeting we frequented together so we saw each other every Tuesday night. Which for the most part I did not mind. I didn't hate Louis, matter of fact I cared for him deeply. I just could not be his wife any longer.

I went on with my life and suppressed the feeling of sadness that I felt. Even after all my weeks of therapy and my years in AA I was not very good at feeling my feelings. The thing I had not really come to grips with was that if I did not feel my real sadness I could not feel my real happiness. I was cutting myself short every time.

I acted as if I was happy. I surrounded myself with a new group of friends. Friends I could laugh with and tell stories to and life felt interesting again. I traveled to the city once a week and sometimes I would stay for the night and enjoy the city life with other writers from the paper. I did love the attention I was once again getting from men; it seemed like they all wanted to flirt with me. I did not date though, I was enjoying my new found freedom.

My hair was not as long as I use to wear it but my eyes were bright again and I developed a beautiful smile. Thanks to all the therapy with Ruth I seemed to be free of feelings of anger and loneliness and I was becoming the woman I wanted to be.

I was now only seeing Ruth occasionally because I was feeling confident and my self esteem had returned. I even started thinking about doing some things that I had longed to do, like learning a new language and riding my own motorcycle.

I planned to get a set of tapes that I would listen to in the car as I traveled to the city and I looked into signing up for the Rider Safety course at the local community college. I wasn't sure if my brain was ready for a new language and riding my own motorcycle was probably the biggest fear of my life.

Ruth had taught me how important it would be for me to challenge myself and to walk through my fears. I knew she was right but I decided to procrastinate on both activities for the time being and concentrate on my work. Now that I was more self confident and free of the stress of my failed marriage I started writing my column with a new view of the world and it took on a new level of substance and depth. My editor was happy with my work and offered me the opportunity to write some other occasional pieces. Life was fabulous, I was fabulous.

Chapter 42

As the months passed I had once again settled into single life which had taken on an air of serenity and peace. My life seemed to free of any noticeable stress except for the weekly deadlines at the paper and the traffic in San Francisco. I made a decision to not drive to the city as often and I set up an office in the small city I lived in. My new office was in one of the renovated office buildings in the downtown area.

Downtown which was three blocks long and four blocks wide had undergone a complete change over in the past five years and now there were gourmet restaurants, wine bars, and boutiques taking up residence in the old buildings. It had become quite exciting for a small city and people would travel from San Francisco and Los Angeles to visit for the weekend. Our little city had grown up and so had I.

One Thursday I was coming out of my office and I ran into a friend, Bob, from one of the other offices in the building and he introduced me to one of his colleagues, Jerod, who was visiting from San Diego. We chatted briefly and I welcomed him to our city and went about my day.

Later that evening I bumped into them again when I was picking up my "to go" order from my favorite restaurant. Jerod smiled and greeted me warmly and Bob invited me to join them. I told them that I had a deadline to meet and that I would take a rain check. Jerod expressed his disappointment at my not joining them and kissed my hand as he said "till next time." I was quite taken by his gracious gesture and left the restaurant without my food. It was embarrassing when I had to go back in for my package. I smiled nervously at both of them and waved.

Later that evening I had to go back to my office for some research papers I had left on my fax machine. It was a beautiful April night and I decided to walk to the office from my house which was about twenty blocks away. As I walked along Main Street past all the new and established restaurants and bars I looked in the windows at the patrons laughing, talking, eating and drinking and l had a moment of loneliness which I immediately pushed down inside of me and reassured myself that I was better off alone.

I was almost to my office when I walked by Henry's on the Park a very fashionable new bar that overlooked the park. There were small tables set out front where people could smoke and there was standing room only. I suddenly felt a warm hand on mine. I looked up to find Jerod standing there smiling at me. "We meet again beautiful lady" he said as he kissed my hand. A warm feeling overtook me as I looked into his handsome face. He had such a charming smile and the most stunning green eyes. I know I was blushing and I was speechless, then Bob suddenly appeared next to us, "how did you know we were here, did you decide to join us for a drink?"

"No, I was just on my way to the office when Jerod" I started to say and was cut off by Jerod's voice saying, "the office! It's nine PM. Join us, please". His pleading was genuine I was sure, but I was afraid to give into it. I expressed my apologies once again and started to leave when Jerod gently put his hand on my shoulder and lifted my hair and kissed me on my neck. A feeling of excitement shot through my whole body, my knees went week and my nipples got hard. I just stood there for a moment and then I continued towards my office without a word. I could hear Jerod and Bob both saying goodbye to me but I could not summon the strength to say goodbye to them.

By the time I got into my office I fell into my desk chair and said out loud "what was that!" After sitting there for a moment I decided not to pay attention to what I was feeling and that I would just finish my column while I was in the office and then go home to bed where I was safe.

Safe! When had I become so fearful, when had I become so afraid of my own feelings. I did not want to go through my life without feelings, I did not really want to be safe and have a small closed life. I wanted to live. I wanted to desire and be desired and yet it scared me for the first time that I could remember.

I finished my column about midnight and called a cab to take me home. I could not fall asleep though, I could not stop thinking about Jerod's kiss. It felt so good. It had been so long since someone kissed me, since I allowed myself to be kissed.

His kiss was so surprising, so moving, so romantic, so exciting and I wanted more. I wanted him to hold me and touch me. I wanted him to desire me and penetrate me. I wanted him to whisper in my ear all the words I longed to hear. I wanted to feel alive once again. The way Paul and Michael made me feel alive.

Up until that kiss I had not realized that I was dying. Memories flooded back into my brain, I was confused, I wanted to be wanted and yet I was afraid to give into it again. I told myself to let it go, forget about it, but I could not. It continued to haunt me for the rest of the night. Friday morning about seven I finally fell asleep and slept until noon.

I had to get my column to the paper by two so I jumped in the shower, dressed in a pair of jeans and a t-shirt and headed for my office. I wanted to re-read my column before sending it off as I was not sure what I had actually written the night before. It was actually good though, it had substance and depth and feeling, which really surprised me. Maybe I needed to be stirred up once in a while.

After hitting the send button on the fax machine I sat at my desk and closed my eyes and thought about the kiss once more. My hands moved into my lap and I ran them down the length of my thighs as my head filled with thoughts of Jerod kissing every square inch of my body.

I was lost in thought when I was suddenly jolted back to reality by a knock on my office door. I got up and opened the door to find Jerod standing there with a big bouquet of white and yellow daisies in his hand. "These are for you because you are the most beautiful red-head I know!" he said with a big smile on his face.

"Thank you. You are too kind." I said as I took the bouquet from him. His black hair was brushed back away from his face and his big green eyes were sparkling with joy.

"Are you free for dinner tonight?" he asked. "I am sorry but I have plans with a friend tonight." I said.

"Can I change your mind?"

"No, I am afraid not."

"Can I call your friend and change his mind."

"What makes you think I have plans with a man."

"Because you are so beautiful."

"Thank you, but no the plans cannot be changed."

"Here is my cell number in case you get free early enough to have a drink with me" he said as he pressed a business card into the palm of my hand and walked out the door.

I shoved the card into my pocket, grabbed the daisies and walked out into the warmth of the afternoon sun. I carried the daisies home and put them in a vase which I placed next to my bed. It had been years since a man had given me flowers and I wanted to savor every minute of their short life.

Chapter 43

I had dinner with my friend Marti and we went to the Friday night AA meeting afterwards. The meeting ended at nine and I dropped Marti back at her place and called Jerod from my cell phone before I pulled away from the curb.

He was at Henry's and said he had been waiting for my call. I told him I would meet him in forty minutes. I needed time to go home and change into something a little sexier than the jeans and shirt I had on.

I was frantic as I searched through my closet for just the right thing. I finally decided on my black bra and panties with the embroidered roses and a simple black sleeveless dress. I put on a pair of thigh high stockings and black heels.

I walked into Henry's and Jerod was sitting at the end of the bar with two drinks in front of him. He saw me coming towards him and stood up. When I got close he took my hand and gave me a tender kiss on my cheek. I sat down on the bar stool and he said "I ordered this drink for you." My reply was "I don't drink." He then said "but this is a special drink." "I don't drink." I repeated. "Why don't you drink?" Jerod asked. "I am an alcoholic." I said. Jerod then pushed the glass away and ordered a club soda for me.

We sat and talked for a while and then we went outside into the warm night air. Jerod lit a cigarette and asked if I would like to go back to the hotel with him. I was not surprised and I so wanted to go but I told him that I could not do that. For the next twenty minutes or so he used all his best stuff to convince me to go with him to his hotel.

The funny thing was he had me at the very first kiss. The rest just seemed to be a formality of sorts. He was quite a smooth operator and I was enjoying the game so I let him go on. I knew I was going to go back to the hotel with him eventually. I finally let him off the hook and we walked the two blocks to the hotel.

Once inside the room our passion could no longer wait. I pulled off my dress revealing my pretty underwear and thigh high stockings and Jerod pressed my body against the door and kissed my neck. His warm lips touched the sensitive spots on my neck and my knees went weak, my heart was pounding and I started to moan. I could feel my nipples stiffen and my vagina was moist with anticipation.

My arms moved around his body and my hands grasped his firm ass. He moved his body closer to mine and I could feel his hard penis press against my abdomen. The excitement mounted and my weak knees could no longer support me and my body started to slip down the door. Jerod grabbed me around my hips and lifted me up till my legs were wrapped around his body. We kissed passionately, madly, my body was starting to sweat. I could feel his strong arms, muscles flexed as he held me up between his body and the door. My breathing accelerated and my moans became louder.

He then turned towards the bed and released his grip on me and I fell onto the bed. I lay there hyperventilating as I watched him pull his navy blue silk shirt over his head. Jerod had a beautiful body, I could tell this even before he removed his shirt. Then he dropped his pants to the floor and climbed onto the bed with me. I got up on my knees and he pulled me against him. I could feel his warm smooth skin on mine and I ran my lips over his chest and down his arms, his body relaxed and he leaned back against the pillows. I pulled off his boxers and ran my hands between his thighs and grasped his hard penis with both hands and put it in my mouth.

Jerod had sex with me both tenderly and brutally that night. I loved it all. The thing I remembered most about that night was how he made me feel so beautiful, so desirable.

There is nothing more sexy and appealing to a woman like me than a man who can make me feel so very special, like there is no one else on the planet except me. Jerod did just that from the moment I met him till the moment I said goodbye Saturday morning. He never made me feel anything except gorgeous and very desirable. It was as if he plugged right into my psyche and connected with my most secret sexual fantasies. He seemed to know everything that turned me on and I was completely taken by him. I was so sad when I had to say goodbye to him that morning. We could not stop kissing each other. I could not pull myself away from him.

His kisses were so sweet, so moving, so passionate. I felt so lost. Why did he have to leave, when would he come back ran through my mind for the rest of the day.

As the days passed my thirst for him grew. I could not stop thinking about him, his soft touch, his velvet skin, his beautiful green eyes.

My thirst for him became an obsession and I insisted that he meet me in Los Angeles for the weekend. I needed to see him again. I needed to feel his warm mouth on mine. I needed to hear him tell me all the things I longed to hear. I needed to feel beautiful once again.

Chapter 44

I arrived in Los Angeles late on Friday night and checked into the hotel I had chosen to meet Jerod at. In less than an hour after my arrival I heard a knock on the door and my heart skipped a couple of beats, my stomach flipped. I paused in front of the mirror to check one last time before I opened the door and leaped into his arms.

I had on a red and black bustier, black thigh high stockings with red lace tops, red lace thong panties, black ankle strap heels, and a silver heart shaped locket around my neck. I had my red curls pulled up in a clip exposing my neck. I could not wait to feel his lips on my neck, teasing me, tantalizing me, making me quiver.

I opened the door all the way, totally revealing myself in the doorway only to find the bell captain on the other side holding a bouquet of roses. I blushed and jumped behind the door and then let out a timid laugh as I apologized. He laughed too and said "No need to apologize, now I know why I am bringing this beautiful bouquet of roses to you, but they pale in comparison, the sender is a very lucky man." I took the roses and thanked him for his kindness and understanding.

There was a card in the bouquet that read, "I will see you shortly, I can't wait. Jerod." I smiled and sighed. I looked around the room and decided to set the roses by the window. As I set down the vase I got lost in the memories of Jerod's body so close to mine, moving in and out, his hands holding my wrists tightly over my head. I could smell his cologne, I moaned and almost lost my balance.

Before I had the chance to turn around after setting the roses on the table by the window I heard another knock at the door. This time I asked who was there and a voice came from the other side, "Jerod." My heart started to pound and I opened the door and threw my arms around his neck. He dropped his bag on the floor outside the door and lifted me up against him and kissed me sweetly on the mouth. I wanted to tear his clothes off and take advantage of him that very moment but I decided to slow down and let him catch his breath even though I had a hard time catching mine.

It had been six weeks since I had seen him and I had really worked myself into a frenzy anticipating this moment. My obsession to see him again had been a daily event for most of those six weeks and now he was here in front of me, caressing me. I was ecstatic. What was this hold he had on me, I did not know. Why was I so moved by this man, I could not answer the question.

By the end of the two nights and one day together I was still no closer to the answer than I had been at the beginning. The entire time we were together was wonderful, fascinating and moving. The more he gave me the more I wanted and we had exhausted ourselves. He took me to new heights of excitement and sexual enchantment and I did not want the weekend to end. I did not want to stop being the beautiful woman Jerod thought I was.

I returned home from my trip still high on the sexual excitement of the weekend. I wanted more. It was even harder to say goodbye to him that time. I could feel the obsession growing inside my soul. I could think of nothing else besides his hands caressing my body his warm kisses on my lips. I wanted more.

The days that followed that weekend were filled with non stop thoughts of the sex and how much I needed him to desire me. I would get lost in my thoughts of him and I would find myself hyperventilating and moaning. I needed him. I wanted more.

After ten days had passed I called Jerod and left a message thanking him for the weekend and letting him know that I had a wonderful time and that we should do it again soon. I got no response from him that day.

Two days later Jerod managed to leave me a message that simply said, "Hi this is Jerod, I had a good time too, but you are too much to handle. Take care. I know you will find someone better than me!"

As I stood there with the phone in my hand listening my heart just broke. I was frozen. I was in shock. I listened to the message seven times before I erased it. I was devastated.

Thoughts of Rick and Hank and James filled my head. I stuffed my feelings and moved on.

Chapter 45

As usual I just got back on my feet and pressed on with my life. I had lost another piece of my soul. Nothing to worry about, I am sure I would hardly miss it as usual.

Life always has a funny way of working things out and giving me exactly what I need just when I need it. What I got this time was a woman, Jena, reaching out for help. Alcohol and drugs were kicking her ass and she wanted to stop and did not know how to. I remember speaking to her briefly once before and giving her my phone number but I thought she would never call, but she did.

It was early on Sunday morning and I was already feeling sorry for myself as I was making coffee. The sound of the phone ringing startled me and I jumped. Who's calling me was going through my mind as I walked to the bedroom to get the phone.

I could not make out the words from the female voice mixed with sobs coming out of the receiver into my ear. I listened impatiently waiting for her to stop crying, finally she was able to tell me who she was and what happened and I told her to come to my home right away which she obeyed.

She told me her story and I fixed us some breakfast and hot tea. We talked for hours and she assured me that she wanted to get sober. That night I took her to her first meeting. She glommed onto the program with both hands and it was such a blessing to watch her grow and change. I took her to meetings daily and as the weeks passed she kept me distracted from the Jerod thing and I thought I was fine.

What I did not know is that I had just moved to a new decision deep inside that sounded something like "you want to see too much, I'll show you too much!"

My overt behavior had become increasingly sexual and it seemed to be touching the lives of everyone around me. I loved the way men would look at me when I entered a room. Everything about me was sexy from the way I dressed to the smallest nuance. Men not only paid attention to me but they gathered around me and I once again confirmed the fact, I was desirable and that is all that mattered to me anymore.

Jena and I continued to go to meetings together and she was getting healthy. The increase in meetings for me and the attention I was giving Jena helped me but I was starting to indulge in my secret sexual life once again and my mental health was slipping away.

The flirting was no longer satisfying, I needed more. I knew that it would be different this time because I would be different this time.

I found myself searching out my next conquest, who would it be. I needed to be in control. It would be different if I was in control. Falling for some romantic move did not work for me, control was the answer.

After all my years in recovery I was still unable to see the fallacy of this type of thinking. How I was deluding myself into thinking that I could control it. This time I would not give away my soul, I would just take what I wanted, what I needed.

I was unable to see that I used my sex to deaden the pain that I felt and that I would mood alter with it the same way that I had mood altered with alcohol. I was unable to see how I used it to fill the emptiness I felt inside. I was unable to see how it made that hole in my soul bigger not smaller. The wind was blowing through the hole making that eerie sound and I could not stop. I still held on to the illusion that it was different this time.

Chapter 46

I was running through men like I ran through bottles of Jack.

I was crazy.

Most were just a one time fling and some looked something like a relationship as we actually had a few conversations. There were some I liked and some I didn't. There were some that were good and some not worth taking my shoes off for.

All that mattered anymore was oblivion.

My sexual life was a secret life for me. It was like I had a second personality. I continued to function during the day as if I were normal and at night I would search for my fix. I was getting tired though; none of it seemed to be working. One fuck after the other. They were all so ordinary.

I was no longer moved at all. No one could send me like Paul, Michael, James, Rick, and most of all no one could make me feel like Jerod. I was lost. I was empty. I was done. I had to stop.

How could I have gotten to this point again? When would I stop? I was an emotional train wreck. I started to sense that if I did not get this under control the bottle of Jack would be next. By this time I had sixteen years of sobriety and I did not want to lose it; thankfully Jena continued to call me asking for my help and keeping me involved in her life. I think it was the only thing that saved me during this period.

As the weeks passed I stayed close to Jena and she stayed close to me and we worked the program together. I concentrated on my sex stuff and she concentrated on the alcohol. I think we both did some growing up during those two months. I even felt happy most of the time as it was such a joy to see Jena's life change so drastically. She had become a true light in my life and I loved her very much.

Chapter 47

During this time I had become friendly with Greg who also worked for the newspaper. He lived about sixty five miles north and I would usually meet him for lunch on my way to San Francisco. We had a lot in common and we made each other laugh. I considered him a colleague so I did not approach him sexually. As we continued to see each other it became apparent that he was attracted to me but I had made a decision not to go there with him and I was determined to stay firm on this resolution.

As the months continued to pass Greg and I started seeing each other frequently and we talked every day on the phone. I really liked him and considered him a friend. I shared my thoughts with him along with my frustrations and amusements. He was very special to me and I was glad he was a part of my life.

When we first started having lunches together I asked him if he could be my friend.

"Absolutely" he responded.

"I have never met a man who could just be my friend, do you really think it is possible." I asked.

Greg's response was once again "absolutely, we will be friends."

I remember that day like it just happened yesterday, Greg was wearing a pale blue shirt over a pair of tight jeans and black cowboy boots. His blonde hair was a bit tousled like he had just gotten out of bed. His light hazel eyes sparkled as he peered over the top of his tortoise shell Ray Bans. We were sitting on the deck of a small restaurant in Carmel enjoying the sun and each others company. We laughed a lot that day and shared some pretty intimate things. I knew we would be friends, too.

I had made a decision not to date anyone and I had done a good job so far and being with Greg filled some of the need I had for male company. I was struggling at times though not to return to my need for oblivion, the quick fix that fixed nothing. It was always there with me, that small voice whispering in my ear, "he is so cute, just a little flirt won't hurt." I would flirt sometimes and it felt good. My adrenaline would soar and I felt powerful and in control. I felt desirable and intimidating.

This was a foolish game though with nothing but a bad outcome. I had proven that over and over but as usual with any addiction I was unable to heal myself, I just didn't know it at the time. I thought I could still control it.

Control is a funny thing though, once I began controlling my sexuality I also had to control everything else in my life. I could not even bear for someone to move a paper on my desk. I was becoming increasingly neurotic about everything.

My writing was suffering too. I could no longer concentrate on anything other than sex for more than five or six minutes at a time. I called my editor and asked for a few days off and made a decision to join Greg on one of his assignments that took him to The Sierra Mountains. It was a short drive but we ended up staying in Mariposa for three days.

I drove up to Greg's condo and left my car in his garage and we got into his cherry red 1962 MG convertible for the trip up to the mountains. It was a good thing that I learned to travel lightly with Louis because I think Greg's trunk had less room than the Harley.

Greg put the top down, I felt the wind blow through my hair and I was reminded of the times I spent with Loretta in her baby blue Thunderbird convertible.

My memories of Miami made me happy and sad at the same time. Those memories also made me very horny. So many bittersweet memories of Rick, Hank and of course my perpetual memory, Paul.

As we entered Mariposa on Highway 49 Greg slowed down to read the street signs and find the Best Western Hotel. Its location was not hard to find as Mariposa is a very small town.

We checked into the hotel and decided on a room with two queen beds. The room was decorated in early seventies complete with royal blue and green patterned bedspreads and ugly laminated furniture in a dark brown. The bathroom was small but we managed to share the sink top with the usual, toothbrushes and toothpaste. I put my shampoo, cream rinse and razor in the shower.

We walked a few blocks into downtown and decided on a Mexican restaurant for dinner. Greg had a couple of Margaritas which helped him relax more than I think I had ever seen him relax. He let his guard down and told me so many funny stories about his childhood, his teenage years and his early career as a writer. I really liked him and I was mesmerized by his sense of humor. He made me laugh until I almost peed my pants. We sat in the restaurant talking and laughing for several hours.

The cool night air felt good as we walked back to the hotel arm in arm. Greg was still going on about his life and I was still laughing. When we got back to the room we both fell onto one of the beds and Greg kissed me sweetly on the lips, it felt good and I kissed him back. It had been so long since I allowed myself the pleasure of a kiss and I guess I needed it more than I thought. All my stress and agitation started to evaporate and I crossed the line I told myself I would not cross.

Greg rolled me over onto my back brushed the hair from my neck and ran his tongue down the left side of my neck across my throat and up over my chin and ended it with another kiss on my hungry lips. I was getting hot and I could feel my hips rise up off the bed begging for Greg to take all of me.

He straddled my hips on his knees and slowly and sweetly unbuttoned my shirt. With each button he placed a kiss on the newly exposed skin. My breasts were swollen with excitement inviting, begging for Greg to kiss them too. My body was writhing with excitement and I squirmed beneath him. We kissed madly, passionately, I was moaning with anticipation. Greg was moaning too. I was fighting the urge to slip into oblivion I really wanted things to be different and I knew that if I let myself mood alter with Greg I would have failed once again.

Greg removed his shirt revealing his smooth hairless chest and flat stomach. I raised my head up from the bed and kissed him, first on the lips and then on his chest. His cologne filled my nostrils.

I should have fought the urge to cross the line with Greg but at that moment I was completely incapable of doing so; I had reached the point of no return. Greg got up from the bed and unfastened his jeans and let them drop to the floor. As I watched him my fingers fumbled with the buttons of my 501's. I was so excited that I started to wiggle out of my jeans before I removed my boots and they got stuck at my knees. Greg could not believe the mess I had gotten into and came to my rescue. He managed to pull off my boots and jeans with one quick motion. I got embarrassed; we both started to laugh.

Greg pulled my legs up on to his shoulders and pulled me into him. His penis felt good as it penetrated my very moist vagina. His hands caressed my ass as he pulled my body into his with a forceful rhythm. After only a few moments he had me in full orgasm screaming, "fuck me, fuck me."

The sex was great. Greg was more virile than I had anticipated. Knowing him all those months and hanging out together I had never really thought about what sex would be like with him. So far I was pleasantly surprised.

Greg and I had sex several more times during those three days and it was not long till I was demanding more than he could give me.

Chapter 48

After our trip to Mariposa Greg and I decided to continue to have sex and to remain friends. We talked to each other daily and saw each other as often as we could fit it into our schedules.

Early one morning after Greg had spent the night I woke up feeling his body next to mine and decided to get playful. I reached down under the covers and started to stimulate Greg, thinking he would be thrilled to learn that I desired him once again. I could not have been more wrong. He leaped out of the bed yelling at me, "you are so selfish, don't you think about anyone except yourself!"

I was shocked by his behavior and his comments and baffled by them as well. He got dressed and stormed out of my house. I was amazed that I was responsible for such deep emotions and I felt that I had in some way put Greg in harms way. We were able to talk about it after a week went by, but I don't think we really resolved it for either of us. The incident was always between us, for me anyway, from that day on. I ignored my intuition, and we moved on with the relationship. He was my friend and I cared deeply for him.

Over the next couple of months several other similar incidents arose and I had decided to stop having sex with Greg. I loved him and considered him a valuable and wonderful friend but the burden of our sex life was too much for me to bear. He had not embraced my decision and he had pleaded with me to change my mind. It seemed like we talked about it every time we got together and it weighed on me. I would second guess myself but I knew I had to stand firm with my decision.

The hardest part over those months was that I adored Greg and I enjoyed his company. We did have fun together and we always managed to make each other laugh and he was the only man in my life. I did not want to end our friendship but it was becoming increasingly evident that Greg was not comfortable with my decision and he started to harass me about having sex with him again. I stuck to my decision.

One afternoon after Greg had returned from an out of state assignment he called and asked if I wanted to get together with him for dinner. I agreed to meet him so we chose a place in a small town halfway between his home and mine.

As I drove towards the restaurant I was looking forward to seeing him as it had been over a week since I had even talked to him. When I reached my destination, Dos Amigos, I flipped down the visor mirror and freshened my lipstick and ran my fingers through my red curls. It was a warm May evening and I had chosen a pair of low rise jeans and a pale green halter top which made my eyes look greener. My skin had a soft bronze glow from my daily walks to my office.

Greg pulled into the parking lot shortly after I settled at a window booth. The MG wheels slid on the gravel surface; the squealing tires made me look up from the menu. He jumped out of the MG and hurried across the parking lot tossing his cigarette as he approached the door.

I got up from my seat so I could give him a big hug and he held me close for a long moment. "I missed you" he said as he released his grip. "I missed you too" I said with a big smile on my pale pink lips. We both slid into the booth and started chatting about the things that had been on our minds for the last few days. We managed to consume a whole basket of chips and two small bowls of salsa in spite of the fact that we did not stop talking.

After we finished eating we moved to an outside table where Greg could smoke and finish his Corona. We were both relaxing and enjoying the warm evening air when Greg decided to bring up the sex issue again.

"Are we ever going to have sex again?" He moaned.

The question made me pause before I said, "I don't think so, why do you ask?" His face got red as he blurted out "How come you always get to make the rules in this relationship? First it was one way and then another and then it changed again, and now it is changing again, and it will change again in the future!"

I was stunned by his tirade. "Well Greg I don't get to make all the rules. I do love you but I am not in love with you. I can't give you my heart and I don't want to give you my body anymore."

"I can't believe I am hearing this, you mean we are not going to have sex anymore, never!"

"I think not" is all I could say as I got up to pay the bill. We were the only patrons in the patio area and nobody else had to hear what was going on between us. Just as I was getting up to pay the bill the band arrived to set up for the evening. I think this kept Greg from raising his voice to me right there. When I returned to the table Greg was taking the final drag from his cigarette. I said goodbye, headed for my car, and I didn't look back.

By the time I had walked across the parking lot Greg had caught up with me. I reached for the door handle and he grabbed my arm and swung me around towards him. "What are you doing?" I asked. "You are so selfish" Greg screamed only two inches from my face. "Selfish!" I said in a low voice. I was stunned he was acting like this. I did not see it coming. He then grabbed me around the throat and threatened to hurt me. I was speechless. His face twisted with rage as he stood there for almost thirty seconds with his hand around my throat. He finally released me with a shove and I fell back against my car. He then stormed off towards his car and tore out of the parking lot like a maniac while I just stood there and watched.

It took me a few minutes to compose myself. I felt afraid as I climbed into my car and slowly exited the parking lot. I so hoped no one saw us. Greg's behavior was strange at best and I could not understand how I had pushed him to the point of that outburst. I could not stop thinking about him and the possible reasons for his behavior all the way back to my house. I went over and over in my mind how I could have handled it differently.

I did consider Greg my friend. He was probably my best friend. I shared things with him that I never shared with anyone else. We were close. Too close obviously! I thought if we kept our minds open to each other we could actually pull off the friendship thing. It would not be the first time I had been completely wrong about something and I am sure it would not be the last. I loved Greg and the whole thing made me sick.

How could I have gotten to this place again? How could I have not seen this coming? How could I have taken Greg's love for granted? All I ever wanted from him was his acceptance and his friendship.

I went through so many emotions. I hated myself for hurting Greg so badly and I was completely disgusted with myself for ever crossing that line with him. Once again my indiscretion around sex got me hurt and hurt someone else. I wanted to die.

I had once again reached the point where I knew it had to stop. I had to stop. Things were way out of control. Now the pain, loneliness and despair were with me again. The loss of Greg was more than I could bear. I needed help.

Chapter 49

This time would be different. This time I would be different. How many times did I need to hear myself say that before I was serious enough to get the help I needed?

I called a woman whom I met while writing an article about women and abuse. She suggested I see a friend and colleague of hers that specialized in issues similar to mine and was also a hypno-therapist.

Dr. Mary had an office not too far from mine so it was an easy walk for me. She was a small framed red head with bright blue eyes and an engaging smile. Her red lips parted widely and a joyous hello came from her mouth when she greeted me for the first time. This time, I did not waste a minute explaining to her what was going on and what I needed to accomplish.

She listened carefully to me and then said with a less demure smile, "if you are not ready to get to the bottom of this, don't squander my time or yours." At first, I was taken back by her response but I knew she was right; it was time for me to find those twists in my personality that continued to bring me to the same place over and over again with men.

I wanted serenity in my life. I wanted peace. I also wanted fun and laughter. I wanted to stop hurting myself and others. I wanted to be a joy in the lives of those around me. I wanted to be like Sheila and Loretta. I wanted to light up the room with my presence and my smile.

What I did not know was how hard it would be to look into my life and accept all of me; and find out in the end it would be worth every tear I shed.

Chapter 50

Primarily we addressed the obvious issue of my sexual addiction. The mood altering, flirtatious behavior and my need to be in control; which all seemed to be tied together in some way. I also wanted to look at my issues surrounding selfishness as I was still burning from Greg's accusation.

During our first session we talked in general about the character traits associated with my addiction and how these traits affected me and others.

After just a short period of time I was able to see, with Dr. Mary's help, how the way I looked, the way I moved, the way I approached people in both my career and personal activities was really about my addiction and my need for love and attention.

I was also surprised to find out how I used my attractive appearance to gain power and put the men in my life at a complete disadvantage emotionally. They all gave me what I wanted till they could not give anymore and I was ashamed to see how my personality made some of them so tired and frustrated that they had to exert their physical power in return.

Each of these early sessions wore me out. I had to go home and pull the covers over my head and hide. Releasing all the things I had come to believe about myself was far more traumatic than I ever thought possible. It felt like I would disappear, become the invisible woman, which was my greatest fear of all.

With each discovery about myself I was able to see how my beliefs around sex shaped other parts of my personality as well. I did not want to admit that most of my thinking and acting could be a part of my disease but if I wanted to be free I would have to be willing to go to any length to heal.

I also had to let go of the notion that I could cure myself of this disease. I had tried in the past without success to free myself from the grip of this addition. I did not understand that the same thinking that caused my disease prevented me from seeing the disease with complete clarity.

As each session touched my emotions more deeply my need for oblivion via sexual activity increased. It consumed most of my waking moments and I had a hard time concentrating on anything else. I was having a hard time functioning in my world at all. Dr. Mary was concerned about my sanity but she also knew that eventually this would pass and begged me to stay with it. I did.

Chapter 51

By the end of the first month together Dr. Mary and I had discovered some significant things about my early years that contributed to the forming of my sexual personality.

I consciously knew that I was a lonely child and that I had not felt loved by my parents. I remembered that my father worked several jobs and was never home and that my mother was stressed to the breaking point most of the time. I was able to recall that at the age of five I had a very powerful imaginary life; but most of the details were completely obscure and we needed to see more.

Dr. Mary suggested that we try some hypno-therapy to uncover these details. I was very uncomfortable at first about the hypnosis but Dr. Mary assured me that it was safe and that I could come out of it at any time I felt afraid or threatened. She never let me down and always made sure I was safe and each session was recorded so that I could go back and listen to the things I talked about.

The first time Dr. Mary put me under I had a hard time relaxing so she decided to lead me through a guided relaxation instead of a regression session. It was wonderful and I came out of it feeling rested and recharged. It was a positive introduction to the hypnosis which helped me to be less stressed the next time.

The subject of the first regression we recorded was surprising to me. My first recollection was of a woman who lived in my neighborhood when I was a very young child. I don't know her name and I did not remember consciously any interaction with her.

Dr. Mary: Tell me what you see?

I see a beautiful woman with black hair and red lips. She is walking along the sidewalk, passing me, I wave at her and she smiles and waves back.

Dr. Mary: How old are you?

Five.

Dr. Mary: What is happening now?

My mother is pulling me off the porch into the house, telling me not to talk to her. The beautiful lady looks at me with sad eyes and then makes a funny face at my mother.

Dr. Mary: What is happening now?

I am sitting on a bed with a satin bedspread watching the beautiful lady comb her long black hair. She is sitting at a dressing table in front of the mirror and I can see her reflection in the mirror. Her red lips are smiling at me.

Dr. Mary: How do you feel?

I feel safe.

After I listened to the tape we talked about this woman. Who was she? I then remembered her from the neighborhood I lived in from age two to age seven.

As I looked back on it from where I was, I could see clearly that she was probably not a "good" girl and my mother judged her for that. She would wear tight pants and a black leather jacket and high heels. I always thought she was beautiful; it was nice to see her in my mind again. It obviously left a strong impression on me even though I did not think about her. I have always loved red lipstick.

After the session I thought about her a lot and I tried to remember why I was sitting on her bed watching her. She must have lived nearby and there were many times as a child that I was playing alone, she must have invited me into her home, I just could not remember, and it didn't really matter. My memories of her were pleasant ones.

Chapter 52

The next significant session was one where my father was punishing me. I came out of the hypnosis shaken and sexually charged.

Dr. Mary: What do you see?

I am going into my parent's bedroom.

Dr. Mary: Who's in the bedroom?

My father and he looks angry.

Dr. Mary: What's happening now?

He is making me lean across the edge of the bed. Ouch, ouch, ouch...

Dr. Mary: What is your father doing?

He is hitting my bottom with his belt, it hurts, he's hurting me, make him stop.

Dr. Mary: You're safe you are not there you are here with me, it's not really happening.

Make him stop, stop, stop, stop.....

Dr. Mary: It's okay, I'm going to count to five, when I say five you will be with me. One. Two. Three. Four. Five.

I know that over the years it had been a recurring fantasy theme for me and now I know why. I did love my father but I never really felt that I connected with him in any way except on the days he beat me.

This discovery really helped me see why I felt so connected to Paul all those years. It was the pleasure mixed with pain. It was the recognition of my first love, my father. The same man who I never had any other connection to except for my feelings of love for him and the only intimacy I experienced with him was pain.

As time went on I discovered so many feelings that I had stuffed deep inside because the hurt was too much to bear.

I realized that I was a lonely child who never felt connected to either my mother or father.

Dr. Mary listened carefully to me as I would describe different times in my childhood, most just seemed ordinary. But it was in these ordinary moments that Dr. Mary was able to piece together the reasons why I had associated physical touch with being accepted. As I looked back over the relationships of my life, the illusion that I was accepted and somehow loved was the significant reason that I not only went back for more but the more was never enough to fill the gaping hole in my soul.

On a cold day in January I went to see Dr. Mary for my usual weekly session. I was feeling a bit agitated prior to the visit and the cold, rainy weather was adding to my agitation. I had always preferred the warmth of summer to the cold of winter but that alone did not explain my visible irritability. I grumbled as I passed a couple arm in arm laughing with each other and secretly wished they were on another sidewalk away from me.

Dr. Mary noticed immediately that I was not okay and asked me what was going on. "I don't know!" I screamed and then I broke down and started to sob. Dr. Mary sat there quietly for a moment and then suggested we move along. "There must be something coming up, I haven't seen you like this for a while now. Lie down, relax, let's get started."

Dr. Mary: Tell me what you see.

I am walking down the street.

Dr. Mary: Where are you going?

I don't know I can't see anything but me. I am cold though, I have on my raincoat and galoshes. Rain drops are dripping off my hair. I have books in my hand; I must be walking home from school.

Dr. Mary: How old are you.

I am ..... nine!

Dr. Mary: Can you see anything else?

I am walking by my favorite sweet shop and Mr. Johnson is waving to me through the window. I am waving back. Mr. Johnson comes to the door and tells me to come in and get warm, he says I look cold. I go into the store. No one else is there, just me and Mr. Johnson, it is warm inside and I can smell the fresh baked cookies. It is warm by the stove and I set down my books and take off my wet raincoat which I lay carefully on one of the stools. Mr. Johnson asks me if I would like a cookie, I say yes and he gives me a cookie wrapped in a paper napkin. I say thank you and I take a bite of the warm cookie.

Dr. Mary: What's happening now?

I am sitting on Mr. Johnson's lap and he is reading a story to me from a big book. I feel safe and warm in his lap. I like Mr. Johnson, I think he likes me; we both look very happy and content.

Dr. Mary: Is there anything else happening?

It's getting late and I have to leave but I don't want to; it is warm and loving in Mr. Johnson's shop and I feel very sad that I have to go. He helps me with my raincoat and hands me my books. It is still raining and I don't want to go outside. I cry as he holds the door open for me and says goodbye.

Dr. Mary: I am going to bring you back now, one, two, three, four, five. How do you feel?

I feel okay; no I feel a little sad.

Dr. Mary: Do you know why you feel sad?

I just feel sad.

I listened to the tape of that session when I got home and was able to remember Mr. Johnson. The feeling I remembered most was that I always felt safe and protected with him; unlike how I felt with my father. I also remember that he talked to me and listened to me and made me laugh. I remembered that I liked him a lot.

Dr. Mary and I talked about Mr. Johnson on my next visit and she asked me if he ever did anything bad to me. I thought long and hard about the question but could not think of anything but feeling accepted and loved by him. I also was able to remember the sadness I felt when we moved to another city, I was eleven and I never saw Mr. Johnson again.

This memory of Mr. Johnson brought up memories of several other people in my life who I was close to and felt accepted by that were ripped from my life. My grandmother, my grandfather, and my Uncle Ray; all of them had died when I was a child.

My memories of my grandfather were few; he died when I was six years old. Whenever I would see a picture of him I always had a warm and loving feeling in my heart. My grandmother lived next door to us after my grandfather died and I would spend many evenings with her watching television and feeling loved. When I was fourteen she died and I was once again alone and afraid.

Uncle Ray, whom I really adored, would pop in and out of our lives during many of my early years. He always brought gifts, but more importantly, he brought laughter to our house when he arrived and much sadness when he would depart. My mother never laughed much except when Uncle Ray was around. "Laughter keeps you young" he would say. Unfortunately Uncle Ray's laughter could not save him the night he got hit by a car as he staggered along Main Street after leaving his favorite bar. I was fifteen when this tragedy happened and the thought of never seeing Uncle Ray again devastated me. I thought I would never laugh again. Our love for Uncle Ray was the only thing my mother and I ever agreed about. We cried for months afterwards.

As we uncovered these memories we were able to piece together a pattern in my behavior. A pattern which explained my need for physical touch coupled with an inability to become emotionally attached to anyone for a long period of time.

I wanted things to be different in my life so Dr. Mary and I worked very hard to remove the roadblocks that I had placed in my life that kept me alone, afraid, and unhappy. She also helped me open up my heart so I could share the love she knew I had deep inside of me.

Dr. Mary also encouraged me to expand my life; my physical life, my emotional life, as well as my spiritual life. At first, it was hard for me to do some of the things I had learned from her and from my meetings; but I kept at it and slowly things changed in me, and my life opened up and so did my heart.

Chapter 53

In August after more than ten months of sessions once a week I was feeling much better about myself. I could watch myself and see when my thinking or my actions were crossing the line. I knew that my goal had to be to stop hurting others and myself.

Dr. Mary had incorporated healing meditations into our sessions where I would bask in the sunlight of positive affirmations surrounding my well being.

I never thought I could make myself feel happy and accepted. I always thought that I needed others to make me feel this way. I had finally reached a place where I could be fully who I was at the core of my being and know that others' opinions about me were really none of my business. All that mattered was how I felt about myself.

All of my hard work paid off in both my personal and professional life. I had accepted a position as editor for a glossy women's magazine, which allowed more creativity in my work and I purchased my own home where I could also have my office and my new puppy Sadie. Life was good and I was fabulous.

Chapter 54

In March of the following year I was in Los Angeles on my way back home from a business trip when the flight I was scheduled to be on was grounded due to a mechanical failure. I was a bit irritated as I had been looking forward to getting home and seeing Sadie and sleeping in my own bed. I started to complain about the situation when another passenger reminded me that things could have been worse. "We could have been in the air, aren't we lucky they caught it while we were still on the ground." "You're right, why am I complaining." I said, smiling. We both giggled at our good fortune.

"We have time to get some dinner, would you like to join me?" He asked. "Eating dinner alone is no fun." I replied. I stood up and as I grabbed the handle of my laptop computer, lifting it from the seat, I said "Let's see what we can find." "I know the perfect place; by the way my name is Jorge." He said with a boyish grin. I introduced myself and we started walking towards the terminal.

Jorge took me to Burger King, I was impressed. A man who is so okay with who he is that he would take a woman to Burger King was a refreshing experience. He even talked me into having a milkshake.

Jorge was delightful company that night and his personality was as refreshing as his restaurant choice. He made me laugh as he told me tales of his adventures moving to the United States from Spain seventeen years earlier. I was fascinated with his little boy charm and his joyful spirit. I wanted to have more fun in my life and I listened to him with great curiosity. The three hours and twenty minutes till the next flight out flew by; it hardly seemed like we waited at all. I was sad that it was all going to come to an end too soon.

The flight was not full which made it possible for Jorge and I to sit next to each other and have that last fifty minutes together before parting company. I meet so many people on the road; even though we may have had an enjoyable conversation, I don't often think about them again. With Jorge it was different, I did not want to say goodbye to him. He had definitely captured my attention in a way I could not remember; the closest I could come to was the way I felt about Louis, but it was even better with Jorge.

We exchanged business cards as we exited the airplane and he kissed me gently on the cheek. I blushed and then gave him a friendly hug as I told him goodbye. He had such a sweet smile on his face at that moment.

I picked up my suitcase from the baggage area and walked to the parking garage where I left my car. During my long drive home I thought about his sweet boyish smile and his soft kiss. Jorge was attractive, not gorgeous. His dark brown wavy hair was brushed back away from his tan face. He had amazing green eyes that sparkled with a love for life.

His long eyelashes made his green eyes more startling and his square jaw gave him a rugged look. He was dressed casually, blue jeans and a black acetate sport shirt that hung loosely on his fit torso. He was about six feet tall and in spite of the fact that we ate hamburgers for dinner I was sure he took care of himself.

I was so lost in my thoughts about Jorge that I had forgotten to switch my cell phone back on and by the time I got home I had a message from him.

Hi this is Jorge. I wanted to thank you for keeping me company this evening. I will be in the area for four days and I was wondering if you will have dinner with me again? I promise I won't take you to

Burger King, something a bit nicer. Okay, well, call me. I hope you call me. Bye.

I was listening to the message as I was unlocking the front door of my house and manhandling my luggage through the door. Sadie was waiting for me and she nearly knocked me off my feet. I dropped everything including the phone to give her hugs and kisses. We were both very happy to see each other.

Sadie sat by my side and watched my every move as I unpacked my suitcases and put my things away. I could hardly wait to get in the shower and let the warm water wash the tired from me. I also just wanted to lie in my own bed and feel its comfort hug me. My bed was one thing I missed when I was traveling, and Sadie was the other.

As I stepped from the shower and looked at my reflection in the mirrored shower door I was satisfied that I had been able to keep in good shape and I looked very good for a woman my age. In spite of all the past abuse my skin looked radiant and my eyes shined with life. My red hair had gotten lighter and shorter but it was still attractive. I was very satisfied with my looks at age forty seven.

I applied lotion to my body and face, brushed my teeth and combed my hair before slipping into my bathrobe. I sat on my bed and hit the talk button on my cell phone.

My stomach got butterflies when I heard his voice on the other end. "This is Jorge." "Jorge, hello, I'm sorry I missed your call." I said. "I'm so glad you called, can we have dinner again." He said with excitement in his voice. "Absolutely, when is a good time for you?" I asked.

We made plans to meet the next evening.

Chapter 55

As I drove to the restaurant to meet Jorge I could not recall a time that I had been so excited to see someone again. He stirred emotions in me that I felt confused about. Was I experiencing feelings of infatuation, maybe even love? I kept telling myself it was not possible, but the feelings remained with me.

I had made so many mistakes in my life surrounding men. Even though I was a new person I was still afraid to trust my feelings in regards to men. Were these feelings I was having for Jorge real, or were they just another one of my sex excursions dressed up to look like romance. Was I just fooling myself again into believing things would be different this time because I was different this time?

I pulled over to the side of the road along the curb and turned off the engine. I sat there motionless with my eyes closed for a minute trying to sort out all the thoughts flying through my brain. I was so inexperienced at having a normal friendly relationship with a man. It is what I wanted most. I wanted to be normal. I wanted to fall in love and stay that way. I wanted a partner; someone I could build a life with. I felt so inadequate at that moment and tears welled up in my eyes. "Don't start crying now!" I yelled to myself, which made me let out a laugh. "I am crazy!"

I told myself to go and have fun and enjoy Jorge's company, don't overwhelm him and don't overwhelm myself. I started the engine, pulled away from the curb and entered the flow of traffic. I was only a few blocks away from the restaurant when a song came on the radio reminding me to "be myself". I sang along, and I was reminded that being myself was always the best way to go in every situation. I no longer had to mood alter because I felt like I was not enough. I no longer had to be a phony because I was not enough. I was enough. I would always be enough no matter what anyone else thought.

I walked into the restaurant and scanned the small room for Jorge's beautiful smile, and sure enough he was sitting at a table in the back smiling at me. I walked towards him with a big smile on my face and as I reached the table he stood up. I have always loved that! It is so romantic.

He kissed me on the cheek, which was sweet, and pulled the chair out. We chatted about the weather, his day, my day, and some other mindless stuff, and ordered dinner. The conversation during dinner had more substance and I learned a lot about Jorge.

He had taken me to a lovely small bistro in the heart of the city, and after dinner we took a stroll around the downtown streets hand in hand. It felt good and it felt right. I found myself gazing up at him feeling so at peace and so happy. He seemed to be a wonderful person. I was sad when I had to say goodbye at the end of the evening, I did not want it to end.

I did not see Jorge again for another six weeks, but we talked once a week on the phone; sometimes for hours. I was very busy with my work and he had to travel to several other cities during that time. This was a good thing; it kept us focused on our own lives while building a relationship, a friendship together.

I had to go to Los Angeles on a business trip and we arranged to have dinner near my hotel. It was now the middle of May and the weather in Los Angeles was beautiful as usual. I was so nervous to see him again. I had even bought a new dress for the occasion. A simple black sheath that fell elegantly over my slim body slightly above my knees. It had a square neckline which allowed me to wear a simple string of pearls. I had my hair pulled up exposing my neck and I chose soft pink blush and lipstick.

As I got on the elevator in the hotel, I saw my reflection in the mirrored wall. I looked good, but I had a moment of sadness for all the years that had passed in my life. I was not that young woman in the yellow dress standing in the parking lot some years ago with all her expectations and innocence. Life had taught me so much, and it was all about what I would do with that information from this day forward that counted most. Would I be able to stay on the path to recovery and do things really different this time? Could I take my time and find out about Jorge before I dove into the deep end with him. Yes, I can be different. Yes, I can want something different for my life than what I had had in the past. My days of sexual rampages had to come to an end. I had to see if I could be intimate with another human being in a meaningful way.

The next big question was; could it be Jorge?

I walked the two blocks between my hotel and the restaurant with all these thoughts swirling around in my head. As I approached the entrance to the restaurant I saw Jorge walking towards me with a charming smile on his face. He looked more beautiful than I had remembered. His fit body, long legs, dark wavy hair, and sparkling green eyes made me sigh with delight. I felt so blessed.

As he approached me on the walkway he reached for my hand and twirled me around like a ballerina. "You look, more beautiful than I remember!" He said. "Thank you, Sir. I think you look more handsome than I remember!" I shot back as I blushed. He kissed me gently on the cheek and I blushed again.

Jorge seemed to have so many good qualities, and if he had any bad ones I was so infatuated that I would not have even noticed. He was kind, smart, interesting, romantic, optimistic, and he never complained or criticized. Each time I was with him I loved him more.

There was a small part of me that was always waiting for the other shoe to drop; when would he reveal his real personality, danced in my head, thinking about Greg, Paul, Jon, and the others I had given pieces of my heart to. I wanted to do a background check, call for references, check his credit! The things you would do if you were hiring an employee. My intuition told me it was right but I did not trust it. Jena's voice rang in my head, "You think they are all nice, you always like them till you don't anymore!" After all our years together as friends she still calls me on my shit; that's a true friend.

Time had passed by quickly, that night and all the weeks that followed. We talked regularly on the phone and made an effort to spend time together as often as we could. With each conversation I loved him more. He taught me a lot about being loveable. He taught me how to compromise and fit someone else into my life. He taught me about the importance of telling the truth and not being afraid to say what I mean, and mean what I say. He taught me about generosity, kindness, tolerance, and staying, even when I was afraid.

Am I perfect today, no! Is he perfect, absolutely! Well pretty close. Jorge is a well rounded man who has a lot to offer, who is not only beautiful inside but outside. He is thirty six years old and he loves and adores me. How lucky am I?

I am the luckiest girl on the planet!